Sterling's Way

by

Sarita Leone

Lawmen & Outlaws Series

This is a work of fiction. Names, characters, places, and incidents are either the product of the author's imagination or are used fictitiously, and any resemblance to actual persons living or dead, business establishments, events, or locales, is entirely coincidental.

Sterling's Way

COPYRIGHT © 2014 by Sarita Leone

Cover Art by *RJ Morris*

The Wild Rose Press, Inc.
PO Box 708
Adams Basin, NY 14410-0708
Visit us at www.thewildrosepress.com

Publishing History
First Cactus Rose Edition, 2014
Print ISBN 978-1-62830-324-7
Digital ISBN 978-1-62830-325-4

Lawmen & Outlaws Series
Published in the United States of America

Jack holstered his weapon

and pushed himself up in one motion. Then, he reached out a hand to help the prone female. She looked at his wide, calloused palm for a long moment, as if assessing its cleanliness, before she put her gloved hand in his. Her touch was as dainty as a butterfly's, but as he helped her rise Jack saw steeliness in the blue eyes.

So, there is more to this damsel in distress than meets the eye. He hid a grin, not wanting her to think he was laughing at the sight of her indelicate position.

"Thank you."

She sat on the bench opposite her traveling companion, leaving Jack the option of either sitting beside the older man or settling into the space beside her. The choice was easy. Jack sat, and hid a second grin as she reached out and swept her full skirt into her lap.

"You're welcome." Jack waited while she smoothed her skirt, watching like a child at a magician's show as she straightened her pristine white gloves before touching a reassuring hand to the firmly tied bonnet ribbons beneath her chin.

When she didn't make a move to fix her hair, Jack cleared his throat. He felt the other man's gaze drilling a hole into the side of his head, but he kept his gaze on the lady—for it was abundantly clear she *was* a lady. Her actions and calm demeanor convinced him of the fact. At the sound, she met his gaze and he glanced pointedly at the lock of dangling hair. Had he not known his assistance might earn him a slap on the cheek for his trouble, he would have swept the hair off her face.

Dedication

For Vito, always.

Chapter One

Wyoming, 1874

Splinters of wood flew into the air as gunshot ricocheted off the motionless stagecoach's weathered doorframe. Jack Sterling grabbed his dusty brown Stetson and lowered his head just as a second shot whizzed through the cabin. A fast breeze stirred beside his ear. It was a close call—too close.

He would have cursed his bad fortune had he not been so intent on keeping his life. With a scowl meant for Lady Luck, he looked at the two other occupants of the ill-fated conveyance.

Miraculously, the white-haired gentleman had the good sense to keep his head as low as he could given the girth of his midsection. The snub-nose revolver he held in a death grip was old, but it appeared ready for action. The big question was whether or not its owner could shoot as well as he could duck. That remained to be seen.

No time to dwell on what can't be helped. Acid ripped at Jack's gut, the way it had for weeks. That, too, was something he couldn't change, so he swallowed hard and hoped he and his gut would survive the afternoon intact.

He shot a gaze at the other passenger. She was easy on the eyes but seemed to have more looks than sense.

A lock of hair, the color of Kansas wheat after a rainstorm, had escaped her bonnet and hung in a wispy tendril beside her face. Another time, he might have been tempted to sweep it off her neck, but now definitely was not that time. The roses blooming on her cheeks made him want to wipe a lazy fingertip across the creamy complexion but he swallowed that urge, too.

He had to remain focused if any of them were going to get out of this situation alive.

"Get low unless you want to lose your head," Jack growled. Holding one hand tight on his Peacemaker, he stretched the other out and put it on the back of the woman's neck. He pushed her head down, keeping pressure on her until her body was nearly prone on the coach's floorboards. Instinctively he placed his body halfway over hers, putting himself between her and the coach door. It was a stupid move—if he wanted to live, that is—but then he had made a number of less-than-logical decisions these past weeks. What harm could there be in adding one more to the growing list?

Another burst of gunfire came at them from a dense stand of pines to the left of the rutted track. Judging from the angle of the shots and the way the dead coach driver sprawled near the front wheel, the most accurate shooter was somewhere in those trees. The other fire had been cover fire, designed to add to the confusion and, possibly, find a random target.

Jack had been in enough gunfights to know he only had three options.

He could kill or take captive the men who wanted the stagecoach's cargo. There looked to be only the two men, but one could never tell. A third—the deadliest—might be hiding anywhere, waiting for Jack to pick off the obvious two before the last filled his belly with lead.

He could hold them off. Wait it out. Help might come in time to take care of the two outlaws who had them pinned down. Then again, help might take hours to arrive. His gunbelt would be emptier than a creek bed in July long before then.

The third option was out of the question. He had survived too many tough times to get killed by a couple of stagecoach bandits.

"My grandson went for help." Beside his ear, the man's voice was startlingly steady and firm. "My Patrick, he's a good rider. He'll get to town and bring help back, I know he will. We've just got to have faith."

Although he kept the volume low, Jack felt the weight of the older man's words. An image of a pulpit, the man's white mop forcefully nodding to punctuate a sermon, flashed through his mind. Vaguely he recalled hearing some talk about a preacher coming to Brown's Point.

His suspicions were confirmed when the man switched his handgun to his left hand, then held out his right. Jack glanced out the window. All was quiet, almost eerily so, but manners had been hammered into him from his earliest days, so he took his pistol in his left hand. They shared an abrupt handshake before returning their weapons to their shooting hands.

"Henry James Godsworth."

"By any chance, are you the new preacher?"

Trapped as they were in a driverless stagecoach by armed robbers, it seemed an unlikely place to begin a conversation but Jack had tentatively decided option two was his best bet. Who knew? Maybe the little grandkid rode like the wind, and was even at this very minute holding a lollipop in one hand and leading a group of deputies to their aid with the other. At any rate, there was little else to do beside wait for the thieves to make their next move. It was as good a time as any to learn who shared his makeshift prison. Besides, the possibility he might be in need of a holy man's services sometime in the near future was a distinct one. It wouldn't hurt to get on the man's good side.

"With a name like Godsworth, would I have any chance of being anyone else?" The preacher slapped his thigh. With a wide smile, he looked deep into Jack's eyes. "And you are?"

"Jack—" Before he could finish, Jack felt the body beneath his shift, and he remembered he still lay prone over the woman's form. She wiggled her rear end, pressing against his hips as she attempted to slide out from under him. The sensations, as well as the faint whiff of lavender coming from her, chased rational thoughts from his head. Even if the preacher had pressed him, it was doubtful Jack could provide his last name in introduction.

A muffled voice entered the conversation.

"I hate to interrupt your getting-to-know-you moment, but I'm being squashed down here." Jack shifted his weight slightly onto his elbows, keeping his head down so as not to have it blown off his neck while she wriggled from beneath him. Then, she rolled onto her back. "That's better," she said, adjusting the lapels of her no-nonsense gray traveling jacket.

Much better, Jack thought. He stared down into the bluest eyes he had ever seen.

Once he had crossed the Atlantic Ocean during the summer, when the sun was brightest and the ocean sparkling like a treasure chest of gemstones. During the long, dull days at sea he had read or walked the decks, the only two respectable amusements open to a young man traveling on his own.

Mostly, though, he stared out into the water, captivated by undulating hues of blue and green he had not thought possible. The memory of the ocean's beauty had been tucked into a corner of his heart since the trip, a private treasure that grew fainter with the passing years. Now the memory was rekindled, the sight of those turquoise and aquamarine waters brought fully to life in the wide, clear eyes staring up at him.

Jack was unprepared for the stranger's effect. He had counted on experiencing any number of unusual moments, even being slammed by the odd twinge of guilt during his ride for justice, but he had never dreamed he would feel anything like what hammered at him now. Like riding flat-out on the fastest steed—with his eyes closed and his arms spread wide. Excitement, the heart-stopping, devil-may-care variety, mingled with something else, something he hadn't felt since he was a boy in knee pants.

It took him a second to realize why his tongue felt glued to the roof of his mouth. The pounding in his ears, tripping of his pulse and the thought his whole world had tipped sideways when he wasn't looking could only be attributed to one thing—fear. It wasn't something he was proud to own, but it was the icy truth. The possibility of falling headfirst into the dreamy blue eyes scant inches from his was as real as the fear he'd felt standing on the ship's deck. He had struggled to control his trepidation as he had stared into the ocean's murky depths but, in the end, he hadn't been able to overcome his anxiety. Jack had never learned to swim, but he had enough brains to recognize a threat when he saw one.

Fortuitously, all fear of drowning in the woman's enchanting gaze came to a screeching halt before he made a fool of himself. Lady Luck appeared just in time.

"There! Riding over the hill—it's Patrick. Looks like he's got three men with him, at least. That's my boy! I knew he would save the day!"

The preacher sounded prouder than a man of the cloth ought to, but Jack didn't figure it was the right time to bring up the Seven Deadly Sins. He was too intent on watching the skirmish taking place at the edge of the trail. The deputies had jumped from their horses, taken shelter behind boulders and tree trunks, and fired several shots at the stage robbers. After the tense moments inside the stagecoach, the action unfolding outside was almost anticlimactic. In no time, the two assailants were handcuffed astride their horses.

The carriage shook as the older man shoved himself onto the bench behind him. He slid his pistol into his vest pocket, exchanging it for a snowy linen handkerchief. Using the fabric to blot his brow, he chuckled. "Just like I told you, wasn't it? My grandson is one of the go-to-est fellows this side of the Mississippi. If there's something that needs doing, Patrick's the man for the job."

"Excuse me, but may I get up now?" Her voice was as silky and smooth as her cheeks, and far more cultured than any Jack had heard in a long time. His mother had been a refined woman, but she had been gone for so long the sound of her voice was but a whisper in his memory.

Jack holstered his weapon and pushed himself up in one motion. Then, he reached out a hand to help the prone female. She looked at his wide, calloused palm for a long moment, as if assessing its cleanliness, before she put her gloved hand in his. Her touch was as dainty as a butterfly's, but as he helped her rise Jack saw steeliness in the blue eyes.

So, there is more to this damsel in distress than meets the eye. He hid a grin, not wanting her to think he was laughing at the sight of her indelicate position.

"Thank you."

She sat on the bench opposite her traveling companion, leaving Jack the option of either sitting beside the older man or settling into the space beside her. The choice was easy. Jack sat, and hid a second grin as she reached out and swept her full skirt into her lap.

"You're welcome." Jack waited while she smoothed her skirt, watching like a child at a magician's show as she straightened her pristine white gloves before touching a reassuring hand to the firmly tied bonnet ribbons beneath her chin.

When she didn't make a move to fix her hair, Jack cleared his throat. He felt the other man's gaze drilling a hole into the side of his head but he kept his gaze on the lady—for it was abundantly clear she *was* a lady. Her actions and calm demeanor convinced him of the fact. At the sound, she met his gaze and he glanced pointedly at the lock of dangling hair. Had he not known his assistance might earn him a slap on the cheek for his trouble, he would have swept the hair off her face.

"Oh!" She turned toward the coach's far side and ministered to the errant lock.

"Yessir, I knew my grandson would bring help fast."

Footsteps approached the coach. Jack glanced out and saw the deputies, so he turned the handle and pushed open the door. He scanned the tree line, searching for a youngster, but didn't find one.

Confused, he turned to the preacher. "Mister—uh, Reverend—"

"Pastor," the man supplied. "Pastor Godsworth is fine. Preacher Godsworth will do as well."

In these rugged parts, the man was more apt to hear the latter but Jack was not from around here so he said, "Thank you, Pastor. So, where is the boy? Your grandson—I don't see the little guy. I'd like to thank him for bringing help the way he did."

The door on the opposite side opened. A hearty voice filled the small space. "Grandfather, are you all right? And you, Miss Marsh, are you intact? I rode as hard as I could but I worried the scoundrels might harm you both before I got back. Are you both spared?"

Pastor Godsworth pulled the man inside the carriage and embraced him before answering the barrage of questions. Keeping an arm around his grandson's shoulders, he waved away the other man's concern with his free hand. "We're fine, my boy, just fine. The good Lord above saved us—with a little help from this fine man, a gift of divine providence if ever I met one. Isn't that right, Miss Marsh?"

"Why, yes. This, ah, gentleman came upon the

scene and, without any thought to his own safety, rushed to our assistance." Miss Marsh turned and faced Jack, a grateful smile twitching up the corners of her rosebud lips. "How ever will we thank you? Why, we don't even know your name, do we, Pastor?"

"No, we don't." The pastor slapped his grandson's broad shoulder with a wink. "At least, not all of it."

Jack's brain barely had time to register the fact that the preacher's "boy" was a grown man—a man whose gaze had been pinned on the young woman across from him ever since he'd been welcomed by his grandfather. The attraction was clear but Jack wondered if it was mutual.

The musing was lost when a deputy leaned in and asked, "Everyone all right here?"

"We are, sir. Thank you for enquiring." Miss Marsh answered softly. She bestowed a small smile on the lawman.

A wild, irrational stab of jealousy tore through Jack but he quelled it. There was no time for entanglements, and jealousy was energy wasted that could be better used to accomplish his goal. A goal that he had not come closer to achieving, despite his best intentions and efforts. If only the stagecoach hadn't been under siege when he had come upon it... But there wasn't time for recriminations or regrets. Not now.

"We were just trying to learn the identity of our hero." The pastor gestured to Jack, bringing everyone's focus to the same point. "This kind stranger found us helpless and under fire, but he didn't give a thought for his own safety. This brave fellow made his way into the coach and single-handedly held the robbers at bay. We will be forever in your debt, Mr.—what *is* your name, sir?"

"Jack Sterling. And there's no need to thank me, any of you." Jack warmed beneath his dusty hat. The carriage felt close and he would have jumped out into the open air had there not been deputies at both door openings. "I just found you all in a tight spot, and did what anyone would have done. It's no big deal, really."

"Pretty darn lucky for everyone, you riding up on the stagecoach unexpectedly like that." The deputy spat a stream of tobacco juice to the ground, punctuating his statement in true cowboy fashion.

For an instant, Jack went cold inside. Then he realized there was no way the deputy—or anyone else, for that matter—could know why he "happened" on the coach the way he had.

Luck? It had nothing to do with Jack's presence.

He had come prepared to rob the stagecoach. If it were not for his own bad luck, he would have been able to do so—without having to save it instead.

Chapter Two

Had anyone told socialite Kristen Marsh she would step onto the muddy, rutted road before the Brown's Point Stagecoach Station and be grateful for the chance to fill her travel-weary lungs with dusty, hot air—redolent with the scent of horse manure, no less—she might have laughed herself silly over the preposterousness of such an idea.

The irony of her situation was not lost on her as she narrowly avoided a smelly deposit left by one of the six horses still attached to the coach.

Just when I thought my life couldn't get any messier.

Pulling her skirt high enough off the ground to ensure some measure of cleanliness, she took a rather large, unladylike step and ascended to the wide wooden walkway in front of the building. A fleeting mental image of her mother's horrified reaction to Kristen's small leap onto the walkway made her smile. The motion wasn't anything she had learned at the prestigious Boston Academy for Young Women, but it served a purpose. A glance down at her hem made her glad for the improvised leap.

She was in a new land—or at least a new-to-her land—and a move this big called for a few adjustments. It wasn't enough to simply change her name. No, if this plan was to work she would need a whole new identity, one that was so far removed from her real self, and her former life, that no one would suspect who she was—or why she was hiding. Bounding onto the boardwalk like a common fishmonger's wife was a small jump by comparison to the leap of faith she had taken when she left all she knew and loved behind her.

Well, mostly loved.

If she had loved everything about her life—and, most especially, *everyone*—she might still be comfortably ensconced in her suite of rooms at her parents' house on Haven Hill. The salt-air breeze coming off the bay wafting through her open windows, stirring the lacy eyelet curtains and filling her mind and heart with treasured memories. Birdsong from her mother's flower gardens would stir her soul.

Instead her nose felt assaulted by the scent of sweat-soaked horseflesh. The cacophony of barrels being unloaded from a delivery wagon across the street, every movement like a shot from a cannon, made her temples throb. Fortunately her stomach had settled some and the butterflies she had first hosted beneath her ribs slumbered, leaving her slightly unnerved but cautiously curious about the wild world she had just so unceremoniously leapt into.

Still, curiosity had little to do with survival. And, one way or another, Kristen was determined to survive. She was intelligent, reasonably attractive and, thanks to her mother's insistence that she attend only the finest schools her father's money could afford, very well educated. It was more than enough, she believed, to open any door she wished to enter.

A niggling fear that in the rugged western frontier the doors she hoped would be thrown wide might only be minimally cracked sent an icy fingertip up her spine.

Kristen gave herself a brisk internal shake. There was no sense dwelling on what was behind her, or mulling over doom-and-gloom possibilities that might never come to fruition.

If she was to succeed, she had to focus on the path ahead.

In her mind, she heard her beloved Aunt Irene's words, spoken softly but with such down-to-earth eastern wisdom they could not be ignored. *Chin up, child. Take whatever God gives you, and make the best of it. It's all any of us can do, remember that. There's no use sniffling over things that cannot be changed.*

With renewed resolve, Kristen turned on the heel of one hand-tooled black leather traveling boot and reached to retrieve her satchel. It was the first time she had ever carried her own bag but she was sure it would not be the last. She had made this journey without her private maid or a chaperone of any kind. All of her needs were her own providence now—beginning with toting her baggage. Thank goodness, she had packed only the barest necessities.

"I'll take my valise now, if you pl—*Oof!*" The air left her lungs in a fast *whoosh* as she collided with a hard form. For an instant she teetered, dangerously close to tumbling off the walk. Then she took one small step backward and regained her footing, but not before a pair of strong hands reached out to grip her upper arms.

Kristen pulled in a shaky breath, her right hand going instinctively to cover her hammering heart. It felt ready to burst from her chest! She looked up to meet the gaze of the owner of the solid wall of flesh she had just bounced off of—and recognized the man instantly.

Her heart began to dance double-time.

"You!"

His lips quirked upward at the ends, giving his slow smile an impertinent edge. For some reason his amusement annoyed her more. How dare this common gunslinger beam impudently at her?

"Miss Marsh." His voice was as smooth as warm honey dripping down the sides of an oven-hot biscuit. "It's a pleasure to meet you again—and so unexpectedly, at that."

With a small twist, Kristen pulled herself out of the man's grasp. His hands fell away naturally. She should have felt freed without his touch on her but instead a fresh wave of unsteadiness swept over her. The man reached for her arm a second time, but she gestured him away, feeling more foolish than ever that she had nearly swooned right before his eyes.

Get hold of yourself!

"I didn't see you standing there. I, um, wouldn't have turned so quickly and—"

He cut her off smoothly, a teasing glint sending pinpricks of light dancing in the depths of his deep brown eyes. "Tried to knock me down? Attempted to bowl me over is more like it."

"I did no such thing!"

She would have protested further but the sincerity of his gaze and the intensity of his smile dazzled her. The hardness of his chiseled features softened when he smiled, as he was doing now. The cold initial impression he had imparted, handsome rescuer arriving in the nick of time, pistol drawn and shooting to kill, gave way to a less frightening image in these less formidable circumstances. Certainly, he was still a rugged, rough-and-tumble figure but with a smirk twitching his lips and the sparkles in his eyes turning Kristen's legs wobbly, he seemed more cowboy hero than gunslinger.

Remembering her manners, Kristen put less vinegar and more honey behind her words. After all, he had saved her barely an hour earlier. And now, he had held her steady when she might have taken a nasty tumble. That had to count for something, didn't it?

"I assure you, Mr. Sterling, I did *not* try to knock you down. Quite the contrary, in fact. Why, it would appear that you placed yourself between my baggage and me in order to bowl *me* over. After all, I was the one who nearly went down on my...uh, well, I was the one who nearly fell."

He stood at least a foot taller than her five feet, so it was a simple maneuver for him to peer pointedly over her shoulder toward the portion of her anatomy she would have fallen onto if she had, in fact, fallen. The glance would have been scandalous back in Boston, but on the grimy street of the Wyoming frontier it seemed fitting.

"Jack." When she quirked an eyebrow upward, he held out one hand. His palm faced her and she caught a glimpse of the lines and calluses on its surface. This man was no stranger to hard work. "'Mr. Sterling' seems pretty strait-laced at this point, don't you think?"

"But—"

His hand snapped up again, but went down again just as fast. A smile tickled her lips at the gesture. Again, it felt so far distant from the rapid-firing rescuer that her heart warmed.

"Now think about it, Miss Marsh. You and I have not been properly, drawing-room style introduced, but I would say we *have* gotten pretty close in the past couple of hours. I mean, I did cover your body with my own—if I can be excused my boldness for bringing that up. And, as you so delicately pointed out, I may have nearly knocked you onto your—" He raised an amused brow before he continued. "Well, let's just say I almost knocked you down. So from where I'm standing, you and I have formed a fast friendship. I don't know about you, but I'm new to Brown's Point and I could surely use a friend. So, what do you say? Could you see yourself calling me by my given name?"

It was impossible to refuse him.

"Jack," she said with a heavy sigh. Why fight something that seemed almost destined? Propriety could not be totally forgotten, however, so she added, "But although I am pleased to make your acquaintance, I am afraid I cannot agree that we are fast friends. Not yet, anyhow. Why, I don't even know anything about you, other than your name."

"There's not much else to know, believe me."

"I find that a stretch." Aunt Irene had always said Kristen had a gift for seeing beneath the surface of people and situations. Instinct told her now that Jack Sterling was a man with many layers, and with some closely guarded secrets. She didn't know how she knew that about him, only that she did. 'The gift', she supposed. Aunt Irene had it, and apparently she did, too.

"Why don't we take our time getting to know each other? Maybe then you'll see that the most interesting part of this man really is his name." He chuckled, the sound so disarmingly masculine that Kristen forgot the question she had been about to ask.

Jack reached up and grabbed Kristen's traveling bag from the stagecoach attendant. When she attempted to take it from him, he shifted it from one hand to the other and held out an arm to her. "So where are we headed, Miss Marsh? It seems only fitting that I see my new friend safely to her destination."

Weariness swept over Kristen like a blanket. The journey had been long and tedious, the excitement of the stagecoach robbery bringing her nearly to the point of exhaustion.

With a resigned sigh, Kristen placed her hand through Jack's open elbow and rested it on his arm.

"The boardinghouse. Brown's Rest, I think it's called. I'm told a 'Mrs. King' is a woman of some grace, and runs a very respectable establishment. I certainly hope it is the truth, because I am sorely in need of a place to rest." Manners couldn't be ignored, so Kristen added, "That is, if you're certain you don't mind escorting me."

As they began to walk, Jack shook his head. "Believe me, I can't think of anything I'd rather be doing right now than escorting you home. Not one single, solitary thing."

Chapter Three

Dust swirled around his boot tips the moment he stepped into the street but it stopped rising into the air before it hit his knees so Jack chalked it up to mere inconvenience. He had heard talk of drought, rainmakers and ruined crops in the dining room the evening before but he hadn't paid the locals discussing the weather much attention. He had other, more pressing, matters on his mind.

The lack of rain in this ramshackle town had no bearing on what he had to do, so why concern himself? If he were lucky he would be long gone before the place either dried up and blew away or got its rainfall. Besides, there had been worse things coating his boots in his lifetime, particularly during his stint fighting Indians back in the Kansas Territory. A little dust wasn't anything he couldn't endure.

Leaving his horse at the stable, he set off on foot toward the center of town.

A grizzled old man wearing the requisite miner's garb jerked his stubbled chin in greeting as he passed. Jack responded in kind, and then listened to the tools dangling from the fellow's belt jangle as he sauntered away. South Pass City, a large mining town where gold had turned paupers into men of means, wasn't far north of Brown's Point. Idly Jack wondered if the man had a claim there. It might be a good place to visit before heading home to Kansas.

But now wasn't the time for planning trips. His concentration focused on Brown's Point and its inhabitants—one person in particular. Getting a feel for the place, he strolled leisurely just beyond the wooden walkway as if he was just out for a morning constitutional instead of scanning for clues.

Long ago he learned that defeating an opponent was far less demanding when he recognized the other's weakness. It was to his benefit to find out all he could about Randall Brown—and hopefully uncover a soft spot or two that would make his recovering the deed to his grandmother's property less difficult.

Grandmother. The memory of the sweet woman who had raised him tugged at Jack's heartstrings. Everything he had, all that he was, he owed to the woman. She had taken him in when his parents were killed, loved him as if he were her own and taught him almost all he knew.

The devotion Jack had for his grandmother was surpassed only by his resolve to reclaim what was rightfully hers. No unscrupulous con man was going to steal her home out from beneath her—not while he had even one last breath in his lungs.

"Good morning." He tipped his hat to a stout, middle-aged woman emerging from the mercantile store. The skirt of her brown dress swirled, sending a small cloud of dust into the air. She smiled in return, so he said, "Nice day, isn't it?"

"Would be nicer if it was a fair bit wetter." Pulling a cotton hanky from the sleeve of her dress, she lifted it to her nose and sighed dramatically.

Jack glanced at her work-worn hands, then at the

burlap sack she carried tight against her bosom. From the bag's lumpiness, he guessed she had seeds. Most folks in Brown's Point had small garden patches in their backyards, the same way families in most other frontier towns did.

He nodded. "You've got a point, ma'am. I'll keep it in mind to pray for rain before I close my eyes tonight."

With a final blot of handkerchief to nose, she began to walk away. She called over her shoulder, "That would be greatly appreciated, sir. Have a nice day!"

The exchange lightened Jack's mood considerably.

Countless miles, between Carroll's Junction and the Wyoming Territory, had given him plenty of time to think. He had built up the image of a lawless, Godforsaken, thieving town in his mind. Meeting ordinary people living everyday lives wiped the idea almost completely away.

Maybe this fellow Brown is the exception, rather than the rule.

****

Despite an unwavering attention to her circumstances and a newly developed sense of frugality, Kristen's modest nest egg was dwindling—fast. Passage on the coach, as well as meals and lodging, had taken a bigger bite from her savings than she had bargained on.

The paltry sum spread out on the faded blue counterpane before her would barely provide for her existence beyond the next month or so. Granted, her dinner meal was included in her monthly rent with Mrs. King but there were other expenses to consider.

Kristen scooped up the money, dropped the change and bills into her coin purse, then tucked the soft leather pouch inside her bodice. It nestled near her heart, held in place by her tight corset. When she had first stowed her valuables on her person the feeling had unsettled her. Now, even with the money purse further reducing the movement of her chest, it felt as natural as the rib-crushing undergarment did.

Until she was more firmly on her feet, and certain of her safety in this frontier town, she planned to keep her cash right at hand. That way she would be ready to flee if her pursuers tracked her down.

Maybe one day, if she were lucky, she might be able to shed both strictures.

Chin up. She grabbed her bonnet and put it on her head. *That's what Aunt Irene would say right about now.*

Opening the door with one hand while she adjusted the bow beneath her chin with the other, Kristen hurried from the room and down the staircase. No one saw her leave, and she was grateful that the boardinghouse seemed deserted. It saved her from having to make idle conversation, a task she did not feel up to now. There were too many other issues on her mind for her to stop to discuss the weather.

The morning's dry heat slapped her cheeks. Recognizing hesitation as an adversary rather than an ally, Kristen did not let the stifling air deter her from her errand.

She hurried down the wide steps onto the wooden boardwalk and turned resolutely toward Brown's Bank. A telegraph, folded neatly inside her money purse, assured her that upon her arrival one Mr. Randall

Brown would be at her service, ready to accommodate both her financial and employment needs. At this moment her meager finances were hardly in need of accommodating but she fully intended to secure a promised position at the local schoolhouse.

Her boot heels *clack-clack-clacked* against the worn wood as she made her way past a steady stream of people. The braying of a miner's persnickety mule, its feet planted stubbornly in the center of the street, momentarily caught Kristen's interest. She watched, amused by the spectacle. There weren't many mules—especially ones obviously intent on taking bites from their owners' hats—on Boston's streets.

Had Jack not spoken, instantly capturing her attention, Kristen would have probably slammed into him—again. But he did speak, so she turned to face him and avoided an embarrassing situation.

"Good morning, Miss Marsh."

Kristen's gaze met his and for a heartbeat she couldn't speak. The dark richness of his eyes encouraged her to linger beneath his stare.

She felt pulled by the man in a way she could not begin to explain. The attraction both intrigued and frightened her. It wouldn't do to form attachments to anyone given her situation. Who could tell when she would be found, or have to flee?

Still, Kristen could not resist Jack Sterling's magnetism. She smiled broadly, her corset suddenly tighter and the air degrees hotter, and tipped her head slightly.

"Good morning, Jack."

Chapter Four

Years spent at his grandfather's side during business negotiations had honed Jack's ability to size people up. While he tried never to jump to conclusions, it was a rare occasion when he could not at least formulate an accurate character evaluation in pretty short order. *Gut instinct*, his grandfather had called it. He always assured Jack that following his gut's instincts would serve him well in both his business and personal endeavors.

Thus far, Jack's grandfather had been correct.

Jack's gut—or his mind, for that matter—had not stopped hammering at him since the moment he met Miss Marsh. That selfsame area alerted him to the lovely woman's approach. His stomach took a queer lurch just moments before he heard her footsteps.

The world fell away during the scant seconds before he greeted her. Her natural beauty seemed out of place amidst the dust, grime and hardened citizens swirling around them. She looked delicate but Jack had already surmised that hidden beneath her ruffled petticoats was a spine of steel.

And, for a reason he could not put his finger on, he sensed she had a secret—or two or three, even—hidden from view. Discovering the mystery of Kristen Marsh was high on his list of priorities. It shouldn't be, he knew, not with the deed fiasco hanging over his head.

Still, his interest was piqued and with each chance meeting his attraction for the woman grew.

His gut tightened now as she lifted her gaze and he fell effortlessly under the spell of her aquamarine eyes.

How could it be that one small woman could bring such a powerful response—with barely a glance?

A question for the ages, Jack thought with a wry smile.

"We seem to have a propensity for bumping into each other, don't we?" He could not resist the bit of teasing, and was delighted when it brought a fast flush to her smooth cheeks.

"We do." A small shrug brought her slender shoulders nearly to the lowest edge of her bonnet.

A foolish thought swept through Jack's mind, and for an instant, he was tempted to push the bonnet back on her head just so he could get a glimpse of her hair and be reminded of endless glowing acres of prized Kansas wheat. Of their own volition, his fingers uncurled, his wrist came up slightly and he began to reach for what lay so close—yet so far. Before he could make a fool of himself, her voice brought him pleasantly back to reality.

"At least this morning you're not insinuating that I'm trying to topple you into the street." Miss Marsh's eyes twinkled mischievously. She lifted her chin, daring him without words to deny he had done just that yesterday.

A woman with spirit appealed to Jack's tastes. He had never been content to keep company with someone who smiled at every word from his mouth or agreed with all of his ideas. Beauty paired with intelligence was what he had always yearned for in a partner. Thus far, he had not found a woman who appealed to him and possessed both traits—until now. It was patently clear that the woman standing before him, grinning up so sweetly at him, had both those qualities—and a whole lot more, if he read her right.

"Ahem... Well, yes, I did do that, didn't I? Accusing you of, ah..."

"'Bowling' you over, those were the words you used, I believe."

Spirited, and fast thinking. His smile broadened as he rose to the challenge.

"I did say that, didn't I?"

"That's exactly what you said. I wouldn't forget something so...so...so inflammatory."

"Inflammatory? Was I truly that out of line?"

Her attempt to pull her features into some semblance of bland seriousness enchanted him. Jack made a mental note to engage in future verbal parries with her, if only to watch her expressions change during the interplay.

"I fear it is so, Jack. You were quite inflammatory, I believe."

He tilted his head to one side, hoping he looked at least a tad remorseful. Keeping his grin in check was difficult, especially considering the fact that he wanted nothing more than to throw his head back and laugh aloud. By God, Kristen Marsh was delightful! Where had she been all these years? And, more importantly, now that they were acquainted, how was he going to get closer to the woman? She intrigued him as no other ever had.

"I humbly beg your forgiveness, Miss Marsh. I don't know what has come over me these past few days. My only excuse is that I've been captured by the spirit of this untamed land—a sad excuse for any man to justify his inattention to the social niceties, as I'm sure you realize." A fast wink as he swept his hat from his head earned Jack another satisfying blush.

Spurred on by the reaction to their little game, he clapped his hat over his chest and dropped his chin to his chest. His gaze dropped to his toes but he held it there for only a second before he raised his head. "It's a good thing for me my grandmother isn't here to see the downfall of my manners. She taught me better than to impugn a lady's reputation. Why, I do believe she would be mightily ashamed of me if she were here."

Miss Marsh's expression sobered instantly. "Oh. I am sorry for your loss. And your grandmother wouldn't be ashamed—not at all—because you really didn't harm my reputation."

Now Jack gave in to his desire to tilt his head back and laugh. Her solemn countenance was just as charming as her ordinarily cheerful one was.

"Now I've really got something to apologize for." Jack wiped the back of a hand over his eyes before settling his hat back in place. The sun's glare was hotter than the inside of a boiling teakettle. Just a few uncovered moments brought an unwelcome stickiness to his head. "It seems I've given you the wrong impression about my dear grandmother. She isn't deceased, merely back home."

Understanding dawned in the enchanting eyes.

"Where exactly is home?"

"Kansas. Carroll's Junction, to be exact." He waited for any spark of recognition at the mention of his hometown. When none came, Jack continued.

"Have you ever been to Kansas?"

A fast headshake accompanied the denial. "No, I haven't. I have heard it's a beautiful place, though."

"Green pastures. Blue skies." He glanced at the wispy tendril that brushed her left eyebrow. "Gorgeous golden wheat fields. The sort of place that sears itself into a man's soul."

"Why did you leave, then? It's apparent your heart is still back in Kansas."

Annoyance pushed enjoyment to one side as he recalled the reason for his being in Wyoming. Before he could formulate a suitable answer, a new round of braying came from the still immobile mule in the street.

"Oh!" A gasp as the beast snatched the miner's hat off his head. "Look at that!"

Jack was amused. No one rushed to assist the aggravated man who attempted—unsuccessfully—to reclaim his hat.

"Betsy! You ornery old mule, give me that!" The miner lunged but the mule turned her huge head, keeping the prize just beyond the man's reach. He waved a fist above his own hatless head. "Why can't you be like other mules? Why in tarnation can't you just do as you're told, without giving me so much trouble?"

The crowd chuckled when Betsy snorted a reply. The motion sent the brim of the man's hat flapping, which added to the hilarity of the street spectacle.

"Looks like Betsy's a handful, doesn't it?"

An unladylike snort, oh-so soft but still discernible, escaped his companion. It had been a long time since anyone surprised him, but the way her mouth drew into a thin line, lack of amusement over the mule's behavior evident, came as a bit of a shock. Everyone around them openly laughed, or at least smiled, but she was definitely not entertained.

"A handful? Why?"

The intensity of her eyes reminded him of stormy seas. Her displeasure vexed him, so he attempted to lighten her mood with a glib reply.

"It's obvious, isn't it? Betsy's giving that poor fellow fits—and all because she won't do as she's told."

He received a snort of derision in reply. This time, she made no bones about her feelings by trying to subdue her reaction.

Her glare seemed hotter than the sun's.

"'Won't do as she's told'?" The words fell like bricks. "Maybe if she was asked to do something she might be more agreeable. But why should she simply 'do as she's told'—when it's apparent the poor, sweet thing wants to do something completely different from what is being forced upon her? Why should any woman do as she's told, just because some man tells her to do something? It makes no sense, not in this day and age! Why, aren't we women endowed with the very same— and often far superior, if I may be so bold to add— intellects as men are? Why, then, should we—"

The tirade came to a screeching halt. Twin blossoms of color bloomed on her cheeks. Her gloved hands clasped at her slim waist.

He waited a short measure without speaking. When he thought she might be composed enough to continue, Jack said softly, "We were talking about a *mule* here, weren't we, Miss Marsh?"

Her gaze met his, and confirmed his suspicions. Written in the blue eyes he saw the truth, as plainly and as vibrant as the sky above. The speech had not been over an animal, but had a more personal bearing. He waited again, hoping she might elaborate.

Instead, a tiny nod. "We were."

The desire to delve deeper into the mysterious Miss Marsh's history was strong but Jack resisted the impulse to pry. If he was lucky, she might loosen up as their friendship deepened. At this point, it seemed appropriate that she keep secrets. Heaven knew, he kept some himself. However, the pull to know more about her was as powerful as any he had experienced in his lifetime.

With a sigh, Jack recognized his duty and let the outburst die a natural, socially acceptable, death.

"That's what I thought," he said, resolving to revisit this moment in the future. Surely there would be an appropriate time for shared confidences—wouldn't there? More fervently than he cared to admit, he hoped there might be many opportunities for revelation yet to come between himself and this beguiling woman. Forging on, lest he be tempted to prod her on the point, Jack said, "Anyhow, it looks like Betsy and her, ah, friend have reached an understanding."

They turned their attention to the pair in the street. Somehow, the miner had retrieved his hat. It was back on the man's head, with one conspicuously absent ragged chunk in the grimy brim. Betsy, finally on her feet, had stopped braying.

To a smattering of applause, the animal followed the miner down the street. No one seemed surprised when the man tied the mule to the hitching post in front of the saloon, and with a wave of his fist, left her there.

The idea of refreshment appealed to Jack,

particularly as the crowd dispersed and sent a fresh cloud into the air around them. His companion raised a hand to cover her nose, saving her lungs from breathing in the fine red dust. He held his breath and scanned the storefronts.

Two doors down seemed a suitable spot. Jack nodded to the place, put his hand beneath her right elbow and guided her into the open doorway. When they were out of the worst of the dust and dirt, Jack flashed a smile.

"Would you care for something to help wash the dust out of your throat?" He had meant to sound debonair but the words were much less suave spoken aloud than thought in his head.

Nothing in Jack's previous dealings with the opposite sex had prepared him for this feeling of unsteadiness, this confounded sensation that when he stood beside Kristen Marsh nothing in his world was as cut and dried as it usually was. As it had always been. As it might, he realized now, never be again.

Heaving a deep sigh, Jack briefly wondered if he might be suffering the effects of heat stroke. Long hours in the saddle, journeying to Brown's Point while his head baked beneath the blazing sun like a flapjack on a griddle iron, could have left their mark on him. On the other hand, maybe it was the infernal red dust that blanketed this place…surely that could cause a man's mind to become unhinged, couldn't it?

When she smiled up at him, relief etched clearly on her lovely features, he knew there wasn't a single, solitary thing wrong with his head. It was his heart, pure and simple, that caused these odd sensations.

Fortunately she saved him from having to deal with

the sudden knowledge his heart had betrayed him by pledging its allegiance without consulting him first.

"I would like that very much, thank you." One fingertip swept delicately along her upper lip. "I hadn't realized Wyoming would be so hot."

The opening was too good to pass up, so as they wove their way between the dozen or so small, square tables that filled the eatery, Jack asked, "Oh? So you're not originally from around here?"

He pulled out a chair for her. When she was settled, he sat on the chair beside hers. He removed his hat, slapped it against one knee, and then laid it on the corner of the table. Running a hand through his hair, he lifted a questioning eyebrow and waited for her response.

Loosening her bonnet ties got more attention than was necessary. Finally, she gave him a tiny shake of her head. "No, I'm not."

"From where, then?"

He knew it was a forward question, and knew as well that had his grandmother been beside him he never would have ventured to ask it. But she wasn't, and he wanted to know, so he shut the notion of proper conversation out of his head and reminded himself that they were, after all, not in a parlor but in the Wild West.

Leaning close, he hoped to invite a confidence.

She looked like she might refuse to answer his question. When she raised her gaze and met his he saw, yet again, storminess in her dazzling eyes.

"Easterner, born and bred. Can't you tell, Jack? Why, I'd have thought my accent gave me away the moment you and I became acquainted. But then, you and I weren't exactly on speaking terms when we…um, when we first met, were we?"

He admired the way she turned the tables on him. Directing attention away from her, especially by bringing the close nature of their gunfight introduction to the conversation, was a brilliant move.

The woman has brains, guts and beauty. A triple threat, no doubt about it.

He nodded, acknowledging her point, all the while wondering what else hid behind the fresh-cheeked, bright-eyed female façade.

"Point well made, Miss Marsh." Throwing caution to the wind, Jack leaned even closer. A whiff of lavender, reminiscent of their moments in the stagecoach, filled his head. He inhaled deeply, savoring the scent, before he continued. "Honestly, I wasn't paying much attention to your accent when we first met. But, really, now that we have so many—" Jack paused, deliberately letting the silent moment lengthen. He cleared his throat, then said, "Now that we do have so many shared, ah, interludes, don't you think it's about time you allow me the honor—and privilege—of addressing you by your first name?"

A thoughtful look crossed her face. She studied him quietly, so pensively that Jack held his breath.

He heard the pounding of his heart, clear and loud, in his ears and wondered if anyone else could hear it. He hoped not. It was not in his nature to be so openly smitten, and the knowledge he was made him feel silly.

When she nodded her agreement, he released the breath he had held and smiled.

"Yes. Your behavior shows me you are a man I would not mind being on a first-name basis with. Please, Jack, call me Kristen from now on."

Sitting back against the hard wooden chair beneath him, Jack felt his first true burst of satisfaction since he had left home. There had been many moments of pleasure in his life, particularly in his business endeavors, but there were few to rival the heartwarming sensation inside him now.

"Kristen." The syllables rolled off his tongue, their song sweet to his ears. His smile grew when he stood and said, "I'll just go order our refreshments, *Kristen*." She waved a hand at his display of foolishness, a small giggle escaping her lips. Jack raised an eyebrow and asked, "Something to drink? Or should I see if they've got something to snack on as well?"

"Just something to quench my thirst would be delightful, thank you."

Temptation sat on his shoulder, urging Jack to turn and see if she watched while he strode to the order counter, but he steadfastly refused to give in to it. It was bad enough he had behaved like a giddy schoolboy. It would ruin his image altogether if she was, in fact, watching his movements and he did turn and check to see if she did so.

When had his life become so complicated? This whole episode could have easily happened to someone else, but to him—Jack Sterling, the businessman? Turning renegade rescuer had seemed incongruous enough, but now this romantic twist was almost more than he could fathom. Years behind his desk had not prepared him for any of this.

Keep my wits, that's all I can do. Jack paid for, and then grabbed, the two mugs of sarsaparilla placed before him. *At least keep what's left of them, anyhow.*

Pulling a deep breath into his lungs, and resolving

to try not to make a bigger fool of himself than he had already done, Jack turned back to the crowded room. His stomach dropped when he saw who stood beside the table.

Three or four long strides brought him back to his chair. Jack placed Kristen's drink down in front of her, careful not to let his annoyance show.

"Sterling, isn't it?"

Patrick Godsworth held his right hand out in greeting. Jack grudgingly shook it, giving it a hard squeeze before releasing it. The gesture was childish, he knew, but the frown that flashed in the other man's eyes made the digression worthwhile.

"That's right." Jack pulled his chair out, exaggerating the move to give the other man a hint to leave. "Jack Sterling. And you're the preacher's son, aren't you?"

"Grandson," Kristen corrected. "Patrick is Pastor Godsworth's grandson. He's the one who went for help when we were ambushed, remember?"

"Right." Jack gave the interloper a curt nod. "Well, it was nice seeing you again. Take care."

Jack prepared to sit down, hoping the message was clear enough for even the preacher's grandson to comprehend. It had to be, didn't it? The dismissal bordered on rudeness, but his desire to be alone with Kristen spurred him on.

"I've invited Patrick to sit with us."

The words made Jack want to scream but instead he forced himself to smile. He sat, motioned to the vacant chair beside his. "By all means. Please, join us."

Jack had not become one of Carroll Junction's wealthiest men by behaving foolishly. He knew better than to refuse a woman's wishes.

There were a lot of things Jack was willing to do to ensure Kristen Marsh only had eyes for him. An awful lot of things. Bending his elbow across the table from Godsworth's smug face was only one of them.

Chapter Five

Brown's Bank. Just the sight of the large red brick building, with its glass windows, made her think of all she had left behind.

A wave of homesickness filled her heart, making the bright day seem somehow more dismal by far. Had she had her way, she never would have left her home, family and friends—all that she held dear. However, she reminded herself with a swift shake, she had very few options. Moreover, when a woman was forced into a position not to her liking, she had no choice but to find a way out of the situation.

Looking back would not help her go forward, so Kristen took a deep breath and attempted to admire the bank before her rather than lament what was behind her.

The bank was by far the nicest building she had seen since crossing into the Wyoming Territory. It sat squarely in the center of town and seemed to proclaim that there was hope for the less prestigious storefronts to someday rise to the muted grandeur it so proudly displayed.

Kristen paused beneath the spindly branches of a lone elm tree growing near the edge of the bank's lot. The tree cast a small shadow but the shade was adequate, and she took full advantage of it. As she fanned her perspiring cheeks, she looked around and noted that none of the other women in town seemed as adversely affected by the heat as she was. Perhaps it was one of those things that, given time, a body grew accustomed to. She certainly hoped that was the case, because as she sucked in a deep breath and prepared to step inside the brick building, Brown's Corner felt more like the devil's doorstep than a refuge.

Fortunately, the interior of the bank was cooler than the air on the street. A wall of tellers behind metal bars flanked one side of the cavernous room. Their jackets hung neatly on wall pegs; the lower halves of their shirtsleeves were protected by black half-sleeves and they all wore matching dark gray suspenders and eye visors. Busy with strong boxes and cash drawers, none took notice of her sudden appearance.

To the left of the entrance a man in a business suit sat at a wide wooden desk. He peered over the top of a thick ledger, through a pair of thick-rimmed spectacles and smiled at Kristen. She returned the nicety, then walked over and stood before the desk.

He stood. "May I help you?"

"I would like to see Mr. Brown, please." She glanced at the closed door behind the man's desk. A hand-lettered plaque read "Randall Brown" so she knew she was in the right place. She only hoped this was not an inconvenient time. It would not do to be sent packing now like some ill-timed delivery person.

"Do you have an appointment?"

Her stomach dropped. *An appointment?* Why hadn't she thought to make one, instead of barging into the man's place of business? Back in Boston, she would have secured an appointment, rather than simply expecting someone to be available at her whim.

Oh, well, there was no help for it now. The first fumble had been made, and there was no graceful way to back out of it.

Kristen wanted to slap herself in the head, then melt into the floorboards to disappear, but she did neither. Instead, she swallowed hard and shook her head.

"No. I'm afraid I don't have an appointment." To soften the impact of her blunder, she smiled. It was a small smile, but she had learned at a young age that a smile never hurt—regardless of the circumstance.

It seemed she would be turned away. The man stared into her eyes for what felt like forever before his handlebar moustache twitched. *A smile!* He held up his forefinger, and then turned to the door. One knock gained his entrance. He went inside the office, closing the door behind him.

When the man emerged, he held the door open wide. "Mr. Brown is available, miss."

Kristen swept through the doorway, nodding her thanks to the man as she passed him. But when she spotted the man whose office she entered, she stopped in her tracks.

The bank owner was younger than Kristen expected. In her mind, she envisioned a man of middle years, maybe balding and with a paunch. Instead, the fellow who rose and came around the massive oak desk in the center of the office looked to be in his early thirties. In addition, where she imagined straining seams and copious jowls, there were even more surprises. The man extending his hand in greeting was clad in denim, and looked so lean, muscular and suntanned that it was apparent he did not spend all of his time behind a desk.

"To what do I owe the pleasure of such a lovely visitor?"

There had to be some mistake. This could not be the man with whom she had corresponded. He was too cowboy-ish to be a banking magnate. How on earth could someone whose spurs jangled when he walked own most of the town?

"Are you Mr. Brown?" Kristen realized she had not moved an inch, so she took a few steps into the room. "Mr. Randall Brown?"

He came closer. "Randall Brown, at your service. And you are?"

Manners. Where had hers gone?

Kristen placed her right hand in Mr. Brown's and flashed a conciliatory smile. She certainly was making a mess of this employment opportunity!

"I am Kristen Marsh. We corresponded, via telegraph, regarding my settling in Brown's Point. This, if I may add, is a lovely little town."

He acknowledged the compliment with a nod as he led her to a brown leather chair. Mr. Brown waited while Kristen sat before heading around the desk and settling himself in an identical chair. It seemed odd that he make his visitors as comfortable as he was, but then there had been many unusual points to ponder on this westward journey.

"Thank you, Miss Marsh. That's very kind of you to say."

By the way he spoke, it was apparent that Randall Brown had not been educated in any frontier schoolhouse. His enunciation was as accurate as any Bostonian attorney's and his deportment showed he had been taught well. His overt assessment of her person was neither insulting nor indelicate.

Kristen suffered his scrutiny in silence. She deliberately kept her features carefully arranged to give the impression she was not unnerved by his appraisal. In truth, she was grateful he could not feel the herd of butterflies galloping in her midsection. They were a dead giveaway regarding the importance of this interview, and the necessity of her securing the teaching position.

The banker finally broke the silence. "If memory suits me, you're from back east, aren't you?"

"I am, sir."

A chuckle filled the air. He sat forward, put his elbows on the desktop and threaded his fingers together. The nails were neatly filed and his hands scrubbed. So, even though he looked like a cowboy he cleaned up like a gentleman.

"Please, call me Randall. Every time I hear someone—especially someone as fetching as you are— call me by my formal name I expect to see my father walk through the door."

His compliment fitted so easily into the conversation that Kristen merely smiled an acknowledgement. He was kind, but she needed more than someone to blow sunshine up her dress. What she needed was a job—and quickly!

"Randall, then. Your memory serves you well; I am from back east. But now I'm here, and hopeful the position we discussed is still available."

The banker was not prepared to discuss teaching, apparently, because he steered her back to her history.

"And you traveled all this way on your own?

Without a chaperone?" He creased his brows so tightly they looked like a brown caterpillar marching across his forehead.

Kristen nodded. "Yes, I did. It wasn't as bad as one would imagine, really. I met quite a few nice people, and the journey gave me lots of time to think. I also saw many lovely sights, and took the opportunity to sketch them."

"Ah, an artist?"

"Hardly." While her watercolors were passable, they were certainly not spectacular. They were, as were all her other talents, satisfactory. "I enjoy sketching and painting, but my efforts are for family, friends and, primarily, my own pleasure. Therefore, as you can tell, the traveling was not a real trial. In fact, there were several points I found exciting. Others, enjoyable. Very few were unpleasant. And, having said that, I am most pleased to finally be here in Brown's Point."

"Good to hear. I would hate to think you didn't like being here with us." His brow eased. "Not good for public relations, you know, if visitors are unhappy upon arrival."

Time to push the point home. "I don't consider myself a visitor. I plan to settle awhile in Brown's Point. Therefore, as you can plainly see, I am highly desirous of securing the position we discussed. Schoolteacher—remember?"

"Of course I do," Randall said smoothly. "And now that we've met, and chatted a bit, I see you are the ideal replacement for our Mrs. Handel. She and her husband, Ernie, intend to begin a family of their own on a tract of land just outside town. While we are happy for Lorelei and Ernie, it leaves us in a bind—that is, until now. What would you say to stepping into Lorelei Handel's position next week? I know she's anxious to get out of the schoolroom and into the homestead. Does the timing suit you?"

Kristen could not agree quickly enough! "Yes, it suits me perfectly! I am so grateful for the opportunity, Mr. Br—uh, Randall. Thank you."

Conscious of the possibility that the man could change his mind at any moment, Kristen stood. She moved toward the door, and then waited while he came around the desk to open it for her.

"Again, thank you for this opportunity. You won't be sorry you've hired me for this position."

"I'm quite sure I won't be." Randall walked her to the bank's exit. Chivalrously he reached out and held the door wide, bowing slightly as she passed into the bright mid-morning sunshine.

Every throb of her pulse in her temple seemed to say *"A job! A job!"* over and over in her head. She couldn't have wiped the satisfied look off her face if she had tried to do so—which of course she didn't.

When Kristen spotted Jack coming toward her, she broadened her smile to show her pleasure at the unexpected meeting. For her trouble, she got a less-than-friendly nod and a startled half-glare.

Judging by the frown on his handsome face, the bank business Jack was on looked disagreeable. Had she been less jubilant by her own morning's business, the stormy set to Jack's face might have brought her spirits down. But Kristen was over the moon about this latest turn of events and nothing—not even Jack Sterling's moodiness—could bring her down. Nothing.

****

Jack strode into the bank with one thing on his mind: Justice. He refused to let the unexpected meeting with Kristen, or the quickening of his heartbeat in response to her nearness deter him from his errand. Later, alone in his rented room and more able to give it the attention it deserved, he would try to figure out just what his fair companion had been doing in a scoundrel's lair.

Funny how Kristen had gone so quickly to being "his" in his mind. Jack had not planned for it to happen that way, but it had.

His boot heels sounded like shots in the large, quiet room. Instantly his notice was drawn to two men standing to his left. One looked to be a ranch hand, clad in dungarees, denim shirt and leather boots. The other, wearing a suit and bolo tie, had to be the banker.

Jack walked right up to the suited man and wasted no time on preliminary small talk. Idle chitchat was for social occasions, which this was definitely not.

He held out his hand. "Jack Sterling. I have some business to discuss with you, Brown. I don't imagine you would care for your employees to hear what I've got to say, so perhaps we should find somewhere private where we can speak freely."

Wordlessly the man took Jack's hand and gave it a limp shake. He stared into Jack's eyes with a look of complete bafflement.

The cowboy cleared his throat. "I believe you're looking for me, Mr. Sterling. The man whose hand you just shook is Mr. Griffin's. Ted is my secretary."

One of the things he hated most was feeling foolish, and that's precisely how he felt now. His hot-headedness had made him rush to judgment, something he knew better than to do but had done anyhow. Before he could open his mouth to speak, the banker went on as smoothly as if having his employee mistaken for himself was something that happened on a daily basis.

Jack had to hand it to him. The man was as swift as a rattler crossing a stretch of hot sand.

"If you like, we can conduct our business in my office." Holding his hand out and gesturing to the open doorway, Randall Brown effectively gained the upper hand.

Jack let him have it—for now—and brushed past him into the office space. He kept his back turned while Brown closed the door behind them.

Gauging a man's character on first sight was something Jack typically did easily. It had been a major mistake to underestimate Brown, giving his garb far too much weight. It was an error Jack did not plan to repeat.

Time to take back what's mine.

He waited until his opponent stood behind his desk before he spoke.

"So you're Randall Brown?" He ignored the offered hand. He had already shaken a hand. Now it was time to get down to business.

To his credit, Brown recovered from the slight without overt annoyance. He stuck his right thumb beneath the top edge of the gun belt he wore low on his hips. The gesture was not lost on Jack, who had already taken note of the blued revolver in the black leather holster.

"I am. And, as you were so quick to point out in the outer office, you are Jack Sterling. Would you care to have a seat?"

Brown folded himself into the chair behind his desk but Jack remained on his feet. He thought better with his boots planted firmly on the ground.

"I'll stand."

"Suit yourself. Now, what exactly do you so urgently wish to discuss with me? I hate to be—" He raised one eyebrow so high it nearly disappeared into his hairline. The motion made a jagged scar at the man's right temple prominent. The half-sneer he gave when he paused was not lost on Jack, either. "—rude, but I must point out that you don't have an appointment, Mr. Sterling. Or are we on a first-name basis, considering the way you so informally made you way in here?"

"Sterling will do just fine." The man's tone irritated Jack so much that his words dripped disdain. Had it not been for this banker's thievery he would not have the misfortune to be in this stuffy office. He fisted his right hand by his side.

"Fine, if that's the way you want it, *Sterling*."

"It is." Jack forced his fingers to relax, and then flexed his hand. Every muscle in his body was tense, but he made himself appear calm. Letting this land thief know how much he was affected by their meeting would be a mistake. Jack wasn't willing to make any errors where this banker was concerned. Not if he could help it.

"I'm a busy man. I don't have a great deal of spare time, so if you've got something to say I'd appreciate you just saying it. What brings you into my office?"

"You're a bigger thief than I thought you would be." Jack spat the words. He had not planned to get his back up but the hurry-up-and-get-out attitude brought his annoyance up a notch. Maybe two.

Brown's expression hardened. His lips turned down at the edges, and all semblance of friendliness disappeared. "Those are fighting words. You had best be able to explain yourself."

Leaning forward, Jack placed his palms flat on the desk's surface. He looked straight into the other man's eyes and said, "That's what you need to do. Explain yourself, Brown. Explain why you think it's a good idea to steal deeds from honest families, and then send them off in a strongbox in the dead of night. Why is it that you think a person's refusal to do your bidding gives you the right to bend their wishes to suit your purposes? Explain yourself, man! Then, when you're done, you can just march over to your wall safe—or wherever it is that you keep stolen property—and hand me back the deed to my family's land."

The banker stood. He stared silently at Jack, a muscle in his jaw tensing, then releasing. His gaze strayed down, slowly raking Jack's person from head to toes, then back up again. The assessment was open and measured, and Jack stood stock-still while the other man looked him over.

Jack had to give the man his due. If someone had brazenly walked into his office, accused him of stealing, then demanded restitution, he would be more unnerved than this banker seemed to be.

Maybe he's so used to cheating people it hardly rattles him anymore.

Finally Brown spoke. "I have no idea what you're talking about but since you don't appear to be mentally incapacitated I'm going to investigate the charges you've brought against me. Then, and only then, will I address your concerns. Does that sound like a fair arrangement?"

Jack was not unreasonable. He was willing to give the man a chance to redeem himself by returning what was not rightfully his.

He nodded. "I don't want to turn this fiasco into a slugfest or shootout. I just want what's mine, and I'm giving you the chance to do the right thing. Investigate—but don't waste time over it. My patience only stretches so far, Brown."

"Fair enough. I assume this 'land theft' has something to do with property in Kansas. Am I correct?"

Jack turned for the door, anxious to be out into the heat of day and away from the unsavory businessman's den.

"Don't play dumb with me. You and I both know you're raiding the Kansas plains like an Indian on the warpath." He paused, one hand on the doorknob, and looked back at Brown. "You're cutting people's hearts out, one home at a time. I don't know if that's worked for you before, but I assure you the people of Carroll's Junction won't stand for it. We want our deeds—and we're not going to wait long for you to make things right. It's in your best interest to deal with this— quickly."

"Is that a threat?" Brown's hand went to his holster but he didn't unsnap the pistol strap.

Jack adjusted his hat, deliberately keeping his own shooting hand far from his Peacemaker. If he wanted to he could blow a hole in the other man's thumb but that would only confuse matters.

"Not a threat, Brown. A promise."

Chapter Six

Four days after she fled Boston, Kristen had written her mother a letter. It hadn't been a letter in the true sense of the word. Rather, a hastily jotted jumble of lines designed to calm her mother's nerves. It went, of course, unsaid that her mother would be beside herself with worry over the sudden disappearance of her only child but Kristen didn't need to hear the words to know the truth. And while she had been angry, frustrated and a whole host of other emotions when she'd packed her valise and crept out of the house, Kristen hadn't been so heartless that she didn't take her mother into account. Therefore, the short missive sent from the road.

It wasn't, by any stretch of the imagination, the sort of letter Kristen had been taught to write at The Boston Academy for Young Women. There was nothing newsy or cheerful in the words. Even her penmanship was poor, something that writing on her lap in a cramped coach rumbling along a rutted track was impossible to avoid. But the object hadn't been to produce a tidbit of charming correspondence. Kristen had only wanted to allay her mother's fears, and hoped the note had been successful in that regard.

Now that she had reached Brown's Point, it seemed fitting that she compose a proper letter to Mother. She had no intention of giving away her whereabouts. There had to be a way to post the piece of mail without doing so.

Her room held the most essential furnishings. A bed, chest of drawers, night table, oil lamp and chamber pot, all sturdy and somewhat shabby. The only item out of character in the no-nonsense décor was a ladies' writing desk tucked under the lowest part of the sloped ceiling. It sat beside a small, round window which looked out onto Main Street and was Kristen's favorite spot in the room.

She sat at the desk and pulled out a sheet of stationary. The grade wasn't as fine as the vellum she used at home, but it would serve its purpose. A deft twist of the wrist opened the half-full jar of blue ink she'd brought with her. Then, she lifted her favorite pen and held it above the jar for a moment while she composed the opening words in her mind.

Finally, she dipped the pen and began to write.

Dear Mother,

It is with a light heart that I open this letter. I hope it is received with an equally cheerful, and loving, heart. Firstly, let me assure you I am fine. I have reached my destination and while I am still uncertain whether or not I will remain where I now find myself, I am, at least for the time being, happy. I plan to remain here for the foreseeable future or until an event or person causes me to change location.

I apologize for any worry I caused you and Father. I know I have done so, so please do not try to spare my feelings by denying the fact. I did not attempt to spare yours when I ran off, did I? I deserve no better treatment,

Mother, nor do I ask for it now.

What I do hope to receive, with all my heart and soul, is some measure of understanding. I did what I felt obligated to do. I could not, and still will not, do what Father demanded. While I realize his proposed plan might, to some, seem perfectly ordinary, it felt like anything but ordinary to me. The thought of doing what he wanted was like wearing a noose around my neck, tightening and squeezing every breath and bit of life right out of me. I could not bear the thought, and I pray you take my feelings on the matter into consideration when you judge my actions.

I know you will judge me, Mother. It is something we all do, whether or not we care to own up to it. I myself am guilty of the practice. I have been judgmental in the past, have formed opinions without facts and formulated ideas about people without truly trying to see beyond the obvious. While you and Father taught me better than to think myself above those who served our household, I never before had the opportunity to get to know people—especially women—who come from circumstances wholly dissimilar to my own. I have been surrounded—insulated, if you will— by those whose prospects and situations were nearly identical to my own. That is not the case anymore. Here I have become acquainted with women who do what they must to survive. Lest you jump to conclusions, and think I am in cahoots with women of loose moral values, let me tell you that is not the case. I am simply saying I have learned, and continue to learn, that life in Boston isn't the only life for me and that even reduced circumstances and prospects are far more palatable to being swept into a match I am vehemently opposed to making.

Don't get me wrong. There is nothing wrong with the man Father chose for me—at least nothing I am aware of. He is intelligent, and kind, and will make some other woman a fine husband. But I will choose my own man. And if one does not show himself to my heart, I prefer to remain alone rather than in a loveless marriage.

So, in closing, I wish you well and hope you do the same in my regard. I meant no harm, Mother. You and Aunt Irene always told me I'd find my own way in the world. It seems you both knew me better than I knew myself, and were right on the point. I am making my way, and am pleased with how it is being made.

Love to both you and Father.

Your daughter,
Jane Kristen Marsh

With a satisfied sigh, she blew gently on the drying words. Hopefully her parents would forgive her rash actions. Maybe they might even see—someday, anyhow—that they had played a part in her middle-of-the-night flight.

She folded the letter, then carefully slid it into an envelope. Writing the address she had known all her life brought a pang of homesickness but she quickly pushed it aside. There was no room in her new life for regret or recrimination. No looking back. With an eye to what the future held for her, Kristen stood, brushed a piece of lint from her skirt front with an impatient hand, and then headed for the door.

I should mail this before I change my mind—and before they send some Pinkerton men or a posse out looking for me. Goodness, let's hope they haven't already done so!

Irritated, that's what he was. Uncharacteristically so, but still, there was no mistaking it. Since the previous afternoon, Jack felt like he'd run his hands over a rough-hewn log—except that the splintery feeling covered his whole body.

It had been many years since he had made the mistake of wiping any part of his anatomy over a partially finished log. One of Grandfather's earliest lessons at the family sawmill had been to mind the wood slivers. They went in more easily than they came out.

"Under the skin, can drive a man to sin," Jack muttered.

He wasn't sure if he only had splinters in mind, or if the miller's motto applied to women, as well.

One thing he knew for sure: That honey-haired eastern woman had gotten under his skin—big time. And now that he and Brown were hammering out their differences, he might not be in her company too much longer. The thought brought a fresh wave of irritation.

"Nice morning, isn't it?"

"A fine morning, ma'am," Jack responded. His lips curled but the smile did not reach his eyes or warm his heart.

With a nod, he tipped his hat to the elderly woman exiting the Emporium. She carried a lumpy bundle in her thin arms, and he wondered if she had far to go. Perhaps he should offer to carry it for her? The last thing he felt like doing was toting who knew what to who knew where for some old woman who was bound to chew his ear off but ignoring one's upbringing was nearly impossible.

Jack was relieved to see a young mother, a red-cheeked toddler on one hip, hurrying to meet the woman. She balanced the package on her other hip while she somehow managed to extend a steadying elbow to the woman she called Granny. He watched the trio walk away before he turned to gaze into the Emporium's plate glass window.

The window display catered to nearly every shopping taste and almost any need. Denim trousers and work shirts, muslin by the yard, household goods and even a few luxury items spread across the wooden plank shelving. The Emporium's owners had ingeniously added a second tier to their display, where an ivory porcelain teapot claimed the spot of honor. It was not the teapot, however, that caught Jack's attention. It was what lay beside it that made him suck in a breath.

His mother had left precious few personal possessions behind when she passed on. Most were ordinary items, things any young homemaker might need in her daily activities. They had been quickly absorbed into the rhythm of family life, used until they were no longer serviceable, and then replaced. There was one small box of more intimate treasures that belonged to his mother. Grandmother kept them in the top drawer of her dresser, and Jack had only seen them on rare occasions.

From the time he was knee high to his Granny's mare, one pair of earrings had caught his attention. Silver with inlaid turquoise, they were nearly identical to the pair behind the glass. One strand of sunlight danced on the surface of one of the teal stones, bringing to mind the depths of the ocean—and the delight he felt gazing into Kristen's wide eyes.

There couldn't be any harm in buying a trinket for a friend, could there? Moreover, the simple pieces couldn't be expensive, so it wouldn't look like he was openly vying to gain her affections.

It wouldn't be fair to either of them to begin a romance that was doomed from the start. Once the Kansas deed was in hand, he was leaving Brown's Point—and Kristen—behind.

But a gift between friends? And such an inexpensive one, at that, seemed within the scope of acceptable behavior. Once made, the decision wiped a good measure of Jack's irritation away.

He turned toward the Emporium's open doorway but a reflection in the glass stilled him.

Her back was turned to him but he would recognize her petite profile anywhere. Small shoulders, slim neck and faultlessly erect posture gave her the presence one usually saw in a ballroom, not on a rough street.

She reminded him of one of the lilies Granny kept in her yard, slender and supple, yet strong enough to withstand a lackluster gardener. So often Granny lamented that if her lilies were not tough and resilient, her inattention to their needs would be the death of them. Neglect or over attentiveness were the bane of the lilies' existence, he had learned that long ago.

Now, with a smile on his lips and a decidedly lighter heart, Jack prepared to shower Kristen with a bit of his own brand of consideration. She might care to take a walk, or maybe something else in the shop might catch her eye or suit her fancy. Jack could take pleasure buying anything for her. If he were especially lucky she might allow him to call on her later this evening, maybe consent to play a round or two of whist or—

A fast volley of shots rang out, breaking the newly acquired peaceful mood of his day. They were close— far closer than Jack cared to contemplate. Of course, the possibility of brash, liquor-driven disputes, often settled with fists or pistols, existed but since his arrival there had been blessedly few altercations of any kind. None had resulted in shots being fired.

Before now.

Jack's first instinct made him spin on his heel and stride into the street. A pair of heavy workhorses, more accustomed to fieldwork than gunfire, nearly ran him down as they raced past. The wagon hitched to their harnesses clattered—driverless—behind them, its wooden wheels pounding hard over stones and into ruts. Miraculously the wagon made its way down the street intact, but by the time Jack got around it someone else sheltered Kristen.

Patrick Godsend covered Kristen's slight form completely from view, his own broad back between her and the ruckus at the end of the street. Jack turned in the direction of the shots, and saw a man lying sprawled at the edge of the saloon's front walk. A small group of men ringed the body. Had any of them been inclined to fire another round, their bullets might strike Patrick or Jack, but Kristen was more than adequately protected from harm.

Jack should have been grateful to the man who put Kristen's life above his own. He should have kept walking across the street, clapped the preacher's grandson hard on the back and thanked him. Buying him a sarsaparilla to celebrate the bravery might not be out of order.

Instead, bile rose in his throat. He swallowed it down, and took one final look at the couple fifteen feet from where he stood.

They were untangling slowly from each other—far too slowly for Jack's liking. Kristen pushed a wisp of golden hair off her temple, looking up at the man whose arms were still around her with a glowing smile on her lovely face.

It made no sense, but the annoyance he felt over seeing her with Patrick eclipsed all sense of appreciation. He once again turned, this time in the direction of the saloon and the dead man. Shopping for trinkets, or walking with women, no longer interested him.

Instead, he felt thirsty enough for something a bit stronger than sarsaparilla.

Chapter Seven

"Good heavens!" Kristen pushed the lock of hair dangling before her left eye out of the way with the back of one gloved hand. She gasped, the hammering of her heart making her dizzy.

A spicy scent filled her nostrils when she inhaled, and she knew immediately it wasn't Jack Sterling who covered her. Blindly, she wiggled a hand up and shoved against the hard form, hoping to get room enough to do more than gasp like a landed fish.

At the sound of the first shot, she had been unceremoniously pushed against the bank's façade— hard. Her breath left her lungs in a very unladylike *whoosh!* and she had been covered, thrown into virtual darkness by the gray coat pressed against her face. She knew the wall covering her was designed for her protection, but in the precarious seconds when she had felt encased fear mixed with excitement.

Before she had ventured westward, Kristen had never been so close to a man, felt the firm contours of a hard male body pressed against hers. Now it had happened to her not once, but twice.

It wasn't that a man hadn't attempted to hold her in an embrace. One man had tried, many times, but Kristen had ducked and dodged his open arms so often that doing so had nearly become a game between them. That option, however, was not at her disposal in this wilderness. Men didn't give fair notice they planned to move close, the way a certain man had done back in Boston. Here they simply came upon a woman without warning. It seemed that ever since she had stepped off the stagecoach, Kristen had been running—literally— into one man or another nearly every day. And if she took the stagecoach encounter into account…

"Hold on, now. Not so fast. Let's make sure the shooting's over before we get too comfortable." Patrick took a small step backward, but kept his palms on the building on either side of her shoulders. He looked down the street, squinting against the glaring sun. He shook his head, and then stepped further away. "Looks clear."

"Thank goodness!"

He turned a serious gaze on her. "Are you all right?"

With a nervous laugh, Kristen nodded. "Thanks to you, I'm in one piece."

She swept a shaky hand over herself, making sure the words were true. There was no pain, but she had never been so near a gunfight before. If she had been hit, how much would it hurt? When her gloves showed no sign of blood and she caught her breath enough to realize she felt fine, she nodded again.

Smiling, she looked up into Patrick's anxious face. "I am fine. Really, I am."

"Thank God you're all right. I had just spotted you, and was about to catch you up to speak with you, when the shooting started." He glanced at the crowd gathered in front of the saloon. Ruefully he turned back to Kristen and said, "I hate to say it, but I guess things like this are part and parcel of living out here. This kind of life makes good men rough and rough men unconscionable. Grandfather aims to do all he can to calm this town down, but, as you can see, he hasn't made much headway yet."

"Change takes time. Any kind of change." The new preacher's job was not going to be a simple one. "I'm sure your grandfather will work his good on even the unruliest of townspeople. Just give him time...plenty of time."

"I hope you're right. I intend to stay here with him, and although I know he believes the Lord's got a plan for us I'm not so certain this place—" Patrick looked over his shoulder again, a look of distaste on his face.

Kristen followed his gaze, and saw a man being carried away. She wondered if he was dead, and if so, why the conflagration erupted. Surely, there had to be a better way to solve a difference. Nothing seemed important enough to lose a life over. Nothing.

"Let's just say I'm not as sure as Grandfather is that Brown's Point is the right place for us." Patrick smiled down at her, put his hands on her shoulders and gave her a gentle squeeze. From him, and with her heart still racing, the familiar gesture did not seem bold. "But now that you and I have met, I'm not so sure that God and Grandfather aren't on the right track."

There seemed to be no response to the statement so she mustered a small smile.

Patrick went on speaking. "Before this uproar began, I had a mind to ask if you would like to accompany me on a spur-of-the-moment picnic. I know it seems impolite, and perhaps a bit forward, to just foist the idea on you but I have to make the most of what I've been given. Namely, the church buckboard."

She followed his head nod and noticed a pretty Appaloosa horse tethered to the hitching post at the edge of the walk. Behind it a nondescript buckboard, with a towel-covered basket on the seat.

"Grandfather has no need of it this afternoon, so I thought you and I might take a ride down to the creek. I have yet to see it, but I hear there's actually grass and greenery down that way. I don't know about you, but I'm awful tired of all this red dust. Some green would do my soul a world of good. What about yours?"

"The same." What harm could it do? Patrick was, after all, a preacher's grandson. He had to know—and adhere to—the rules of gentility. Going anywhere with him was probably the safest thing to do in this town. Besides, she had heard that the creek was not far. Within walking distance, actually. "I'd love to see some green, and have lunch with you."

"Then what are we waiting for?"

Kristen took his arm but she needed no help climbing into the seat. It was considerably closer to the ground than a fancy carriage or coach and she practically leapt into the seat. Patrick raised an eyebrow at her display of agility but kept any comment to himself as he grabbed the horse's lead. He went around to the driver's side, climbed onto the seat and, with a word to the horse, they were off.

The ride was very short but provided a drastic change in scenery. Just beyond town's dirty main street, rutted track gave way to meandering lane. Brushy scrub turned into low, green bushes and eventually into a sparse canopy of older trees. Cottonwoods, their limbs heavy with leaves, leaned over the track and blocked out the sun's hot rays.

Until the cool shade quieted her galloping pulse, Kristen had not recognized how frayed her nerves had been. The toll of her journey, coupled with her financial fears, had done their work on her without her even knowing it. As the tension ebbed, Kristen leaned closer to Patrick and smiled.

"This is lovely. Thank you for suggesting the ride." A bird trilled above them, its song like music against the rustling tree leaves and the steady beat of the horse's hoofs. "I wonder what that is?"

Patrick shot a glance to the branches, and then turned his attention back to Kristen.

"A lark. To be more precise, a horned lark. Did you know they actually prefer barren spots to nest? As soon as foliage, grass or, heaven forbid, people encroach on their nesting area, they look for somewhere more isolated to live. Not a very social bird, but it sure does have a pretty song. We should count ourselves fortunate to hear it. Not many people do."

It took a special sort of man to turn so quickly from being a human barricade to expert on birdcalls. Kristen wondered idly just what other kind of surprises this soft-spoken, obviously intelligent man kept.

"How is it that you know so much about birds?"

He shrugged. "Just something I picked up somewhere. Grandfather gets around a fair bit, you know. Preaching in different places, ministering wherever he's needed most, brings the world into focus."

"Have you always traveled with your grandfather?"

"My parents were killed in an Indian raid shortly after my birth. They must have overlooked me, because when Grandfather returned home he found me, unharmed and, if you believe him, completely unaware of the carnage. He had been off tending to one of his flock that day. If he hadn't, he would have been killed as well and I'd have been a four-month-old at the mercy of the world."

"How sad." Her heart broke for him. The picture of a cooing infant surrounded by death flashed through her mind. "Oh, how could you stand it?"

Nothing in her well-ordered life prepared her for Patrick's quiet acceptance of his own situation. He seemed unaffected by the unfairness of his life, and satisfied with his lot. It was admirable.

"Easily. Oh, sure, I wish my parents hadn't been murdered, but wishing for something that cannot be changed doesn't change it. I have only known life with Grandfather, and it has been a good life, so I feel blessed. I know it must sound strange, and maybe you can't understand how I feel but honestly, I don't feel sad over how my life has been." He paused, and then went on. A small grin lightened the mood considerably. "And, to tell you the God's honest truth, I'm not in the least unhappy about the turn my day's taking. I hoped you might agree to this impromptu luncheon. I'm very glad you did, Kristen."

"I am, too." It was true. He was good company, and getting out of town, even for a few hours, was lovely.

They rounded a bend in the lane and the creek came into view. While it was not a huge body of water, it looked like an oasis. Water gurgled over river rocks, and a cool breeze wafted off its surface.

Patrick reined the Appaloosa in beneath the canopy of a gnarled cottonwood. He jumped down, unhitched the horse and left it to graze beside the tree before he came around the wagon and reached a hand up to help her down. She hesitated, contented with her high seat and full view. The breeze cooling her cheeks felt heavenly!

Holding her right hand out to Patrick, she quickly grabbed the lunch basket with her other hand, then climbed down. He took the basket from her before they turned and made their way to the shore.

"It's beautiful. Thank you for bringing me."

"It's my pleasure, believe me." Patrick spread a faded green plaid blanket on the ground. They sat side by side, but not touching, and gazed out over the lazy creek.

The view was peaceful, the company pleasant, and she was grateful for the outing but part of her—a big part—wished Jack nestled beside her instead of Patrick. Remorse over the unkind thought instantly shot through her. How could she be so ungrateful? Heat rushed to her cheeks, and she was glad no one could read her mind.

Make the best of every situation, dear. Aunt Irene's beloved voice filled Kristen's head. How she wished the elderly woman could be here with her now. With Aunt Irene by her side life would have been much simpler, the choices before her much clearer. But her aunt wasn't with her, and any choices would have to be Kristen's alone. Right or wrong, good or bad, the responsibility for every decision was all hers.

Hopefully Aunt Irene looked down on her from heaven. If she was extra lucky, her guardian angel might help her with some of the decisions regarding the future. There seemed to be so many, her head spun from considering all of them.

Time for further contemplation, or for heeding Aunt Irene's advice, was cut short when Patrick turned to her. She felt his probing stare, and turned her head to meet his gaze.

"What?" She smiled at the sight of the big man grinning like a mischievous little boy. "Do I have something on my face?" She brushed a fingertip across the end of her nose. He didn't answer, so she wrinkled her forehead. "You can't just stare at a woman without giving her some hint as to why you're doing it, you know."

Patrick reached a finger out and tapped her lightly on the chin. Then, he leaned close, held her chin and angled her face so their noses nearly touched. "I didn't mean to stare," he said softly. "I just couldn't help but admire your loveliness, Kristen."

She saw what he meant to do a scant moment before he made his move. Her heart tripped double-time, the same way it had earlier during the shooting. Again, she felt cornered, with no good way out of the situation.

Kristen swallowed hard, and then used the tactic that worked the best for her. She stumbled to her feet, nearly tripping over the hem of her dress. Patrick began to rise, but she took a step off the blanket before he had a chance to do more than push himself to him knees.

Then, without once looking back, she ran as if all the foulest ghouls in the underworld were after her.

Chapter Eight

Spurs jangled against the wide floorboards as the tall, muscular man uncrossed his ankles and heaved himself upright. A rivulet of perspiration snaked its way down one chiseled cheek. Kristen wondered how long he had been waiting.

"Mr. Brown! I didn't expect to see you here." Her hopes of slipping into the boardinghouse undetected were smashed. Getting past him without stopping to chat was unthinkable. Her stomach was tied in knots but she put a smile on her face and stopped beside him.

"I'm afraid I came to see you." He removed his hat, twisting it in his hands. A wide white scar ran across the back of his left hand, beginning near the thumb and hooking around behind the pinky finger. It was not the type of scar a man got behind a desk. "And it's Randall, remember?"

"Right. I'm sorry, Randall."

Kristen recognized regret when she saw it. It was clear in his eyes, the deep set of his mouth and the sag in his shoulders. The man looked like he carried a wagonload of trouble.

He met her gaze, and then looked away. "Not as sorry as I am."

With every passing moment, Kristen's stomach knots grew tighter. Maybe not eating the picnic lunch by the creek had a silver lining to it. Thanks to Patrick's overactive romantic leanings, their luncheon had been spoiled so her belly was empty—and she was very grateful that it was.

"Whatever do you mean?" Fear shot up her spine, its probing fingers like razors against her conscience. The possibility he had found her out and divulged her whereabouts to her family brought her close to being ill.

"I don't believe you're going to be pleased to see me when I give you my news."

Her suspicion of the man, and his business, grew. Still, Kristen remained calm—on the outside.

"I cannot imagine what you could possibly say that might cause me displeasure. Why, your association, and the teaching position, are the best things that have happened to me since I disembarked from the stagecoach."

He shuffled his feet. The spurs beat an unsteady tune against the floor. What made western men so enamored with the fool things? They seemed silly on a man not astride a horse. Moreover, there was no saving a floor after it had been gouged by a careless cowboy's spur.

"I don't think you'll feel the same in another minute, ma'am..."

"Why don't you let me decide about that? Now, what's got you twisting your hat into something for the rag bin?"

He hurriedly unclasped the hat, straightening out its crooked brim with a shake of his head. The waning sunlight cast shadows across his face, so she could only half see the expression in his eyes when he looked up at her.

Thankfully, the banker stopped procrastinating.

"I'm so sorry to have to break the news. Do you realize a man was killed earlier today? Just down the street from the bank, by the saloon?"

"I am." What could the gunfight have to do with her?

Brown cleared his throat, the sound like sawdust on creaky floorboards. "The, uh, gentleman who was killed was Ernest Handel." He paused, eyeing her as if he expected something.

The name had a familiar ring but Kristen couldn't place it. She met, and forgot, many people. Her father's business made passing introductions commonplace. In addition, the trip westward had produced uncountable such meetings. What significance—or memory—should this dead man evoke?

"Lorelei Handel, the schoolteacher, is his wife. *Was* his wife," Randall corrected hurriedly. "Ernie was her husband. He is—he was—the man who got shot today."

"How tragic." Kristen covered her mouth with one hand. When the man in the street had been a stranger, his passing was troublesome enough but now, with his identity familiar to her, she felt an extra stab of sorrow. Instantly she thought to comfort his widow. "What can I do to help? Surely I can do something, can't I?"

Back in Boston, she would have baked a cake. Here, the grieving process might vary. She did not want to look ridiculous showing up in the widow's parlor with an inappropriate gesture of condolence.

"Well, as a matter of fact, there is something you can do for Lorelei." Randall's face blanched. His Adam's apple bobbed above the collar of his shirt, then slid back down out of view.

"Great," she heaved a sigh of relief. So that's what this unexpected visit was about—a condolence call! The knots in her middle began to calm. "Anything I can do to help—just anything. Name it."

Before the words were completely out of her mouth, Randall said, "Your job. Well, her job. I mean, the job you think you're starting. That is, because Lorelei is leaving—was leaving. It—I—she—oh, there's no easy way to say this, I'm afraid." He paused, his face contorted in embarrassment. "Listen, I'm here to ask that you step aside from the teaching position. Lorelei and Ernie intended to homestead, and start a family. Now…" He spread his hands helplessly.

He wanted her to give up her job? Before she had even begun to teach?

Good Lord, what next?

A hopeful smile crossed the banker's face. "So…what do you say? Do you think you can move aside, and let the widow keep her place at the school? Without it, now that Ernie is gone, I just do not believe Lorelei can pull through. She has to have something to live for, doesn't she?"

****

Her stomach growled indelicately but the food before her held no appeal. Mashed potatoes, a piece of fried chicken and boiled carrots filled her plate nicely, and would have, under other circumstances, been enticing but Kristen could only just take a sip of milk now and again. The thought of funneling any of the solid food down her constricted throat was more than she could bear.

Life, and its challenges, had been tolerable before now. There had even been times these past weeks when the adventure of striking out on her own had seemed a lark. Meeting new people, breaking out from under Father's thumb, riding the stagecoach unaccompanied...being rescued by a handsome man— yes, there had been many moments when things had been more than tolerable. They had been pleasant and she had felt finally in control of her own destiny.

Kristen listlessly pushed a lump of potatoes to the side of her plate with the back of her fork. It stuck solidly against the edge of the china. With a sigh, she placed her fork on the plate and dropped her hands to her lap.

"Not feeling hungry tonight?"

Julia's query forced Kristen to lift her stare from her lap. She gazed across the table at the woman. The other four ladies seated around the round pine table were, like Julia, dancers for the revue show at the dance hall. They were all engaged in conversation, save for Julia whose earnest expression and inquisitive stare made Kristen feel guilty for having been such an abominable dinner partner.

Remembering her manners, Kristen compelled herself to smile. She lifted her shoulders, and then dropped them quickly. "I suppose I'm not."

One plucked eyebrow lifted as Julia tilted her head and made no attempt to disguise her disbelief. "Why, I can hear your tummy growling clear over here. You might not be hungry, but *it* sure as shooting is."

Covering her middle with one hand, Kristen said, "I suppose you're right. I'm physically hungry but mentally—and emotionally—I'm just much too indisposed to have an appetite."

"Something bothering you, is it? It ain't a happy

face I see looking back at me."

The dancers were rough around the edges, unrefined and ill schooled but they were good, decent women simply trying to make their way in a world designed more for men's accommodations than for theirs. They worked hard at the dance hall, and while theirs was not a life Kristen would have consciously chosen for herself, she was smart enough to realize that most of the women hadn't chosen the vocation, either. They danced because they could and it paid the bills, not because they aspired to work in a smoke-filled room amidst catcalls and loud men.

Tonight Kristen was too preoccupied to mentally correct Julia's speech error. She merely shrugged her acceptance of her companion's assessment.

A satisfied nod sent Julia's thick black curls bouncing against her shoulders. "That's what I thought. You've got troubles. Is it man troubles? If it is, maybe me and the other girls might be able to help. Between us, we've had more than our share of man troubles, ain't we, girls?"

A wave of agreeing murmurs came instantly.

It was a kind offer but Kristen doubted anyone could help her now. Since Randall's departure, she had pored over her options and they were virtually non-existent. How could some dance hall girls get her out of such a tight jam?

"It's not man trouble." It would be easier to reconcile herself to romantic issues. They could always be solved, one way or another. "I wish it was something like that. It's…well, it's worse, actually."

Julia leaned closer, the tips of her curls drooping dangerously near the half-eaten pile of potatoes on her

70

plate. "You ain't…you know, 'in the family way'?"

She shook her head in denial. "No, of course not. I'm not that kind of woman."

Julia had the good grace to look embarrassed. "I didn't think so, but I had to ask. You understand, don't you?" When Kristen nodded, Julia continued speaking. "I knew you would get my drift. Now, don't go getting any false ideas about me, or the rest of the girls, either." She jerked a thumb at the others. "None of us is that kind of girl. We might shake our fannies and kick up our heels, but all that's only for show, mind you. When the curtains come down, we're just good-hearted ladies trying to earn a living. Nothing but dancing going on, not for any of us."

"I didn't believe otherwise."

"Of course you didn't." The other women had stopped talking and were listening to the conversation. Julia turned and asked, "She ain't the snooty kind, is she, girls? She wouldn't think poorly of us just because we're dancehall girls and she's a fine lady."

"Nah, we can tell she would never think ill of us." Geraldine, a red-haired, buxom dancer waved one hand in Kristen's direction. Her southern accent turned the sentence into one long, drawled sound that took Kristen a moment to decipher. When she finally did understand, she smiled.

It felt good to talk, even with women with whom she had so little in common.

"Thank you for realizing I would never… ah, 'think ill' of any of you. I have no reason to do so."

She wasn't ready to totally endorse the dancehall lifestyle but she had seen enough of her boardinghouse companions to know they were good, upstanding women. Their life choices had been severely limited, as hers were now. But at least they could dance more than a waltz. The expensive education her father provided had given her knowledge of the ballroom dance steps, but none of anything more modern.

I won't even be able to find employment in the dancehall, Kristen lamented silently.

Julia smiled wistfully across the table. "I ain't never heard anyone talk the way you do, Kristen. I wish…oh I really, from the bottom of my heart, wish I might someday have such grand manners and talk so good."

"So well," Kristen corrected with a return smile. "And you do many, many things that I am not capable of doing."

"I still wish I could talk as go—*as well*—as you. Ain't nothing quite like the sound of a fine-bred lady to turn a man's head, or to make a gal feel like a queen. Ain't that right, girls?"

Murmurs of appreciation and admiration brought a blush up Kristen's throat and across her cheeks. She *did* have some value, and talent. She felt uplifted, and hopeful. There was no clear reason for her to feel that way—she still was no closer to deciding her future, or fortifying her purse, than she had been at the beginning of the meal.

"Why, you should give lessons." Geraldine waved her fork above her plate for emphasis. A splatter of potatoes hit the tablecloth but she continued, "Ain't that right, gals? Why, back in Mississippi girls took lessons in 'most everything…stitchin' and bakin'…why, I heard they even had lessons in talking proper. Now that I could cotton to…the sewin' needle and oven weren't made for me, with my clumsy nature, but now talking—that I could take a fancy to."

Her friends giggled.

Julia teased, "Yeah, we know just how much you like to talk, Geraldine. God knows, you could talk the ears off corn if you set your mind to it. Couldn't she?"

The other women voiced their agreement, much of it in good-natured jibes or harmless jokes.

Kristen felt like part of the group, if only for the minute. She sorely missed her friends from Boston. Out here she was on her own, by her own choice, but that didn't mean she still didn't sometimes long for companionship and girl-talk. She basked in the warmth of friendship and laughter, and joking over small things. It warmed her heart, and fed her soul. Mostly, it made her feel less lonely than she had been in a long time.

Then, an idea. It was just a small idea, really. Not a blazing, red-hot firebrand of an idea, but more a flickering, hopeful wisp of one. Still...even the tiniest ember could be fanned into a roaring flame, if given the right care and attention.

Suddenly her appetite returned, as loud and demanding as her rumbling belly. She lifted her fork, scooped a more than adequate lump of potatoes onto the tines and raised it to her mouth. If her circumstances didn't improve, she might not be able to afford many more meals, so why not eat up? The company was good, the food hot and there was no amount of worrying that could erase the lousy day she'd just endured.

With a toss of her head, Kristen wondered what was on the menu for dessert. She thought she might be able to eat a pie—or two—on her own. The knots that had plagued her for hours had finally unraveled, and she wasn't about to pass up the opportunity to enjoy the respite.

Undoubtedly she would spend the night staring at the darkened ceiling in her room, formulating the details of the plan taking shape in her head.

Now the ladies had managed to lift her spirits and she wasn't silly enough to ignore the warmth flooding her veins. It had nothing to do with Mrs. King's excellent chicken or the company, although both of those were enjoyable enough. And, thank goodness, it didn't have anything to do with the state of her personal life—the romantic aspects of it, that was.

No, the quickening of Kristen's pulse was the first flickering glow of providence. It was long overdue, so she savored the heat of optimism as fully as the meal.

Chapter Nine

The Emporium was nearly empty, the hour too early for most residents of the town to be out and about. Kristen was pleased there was only one other customer in the place. It gave her the clerk's undivided attention.

Thank goodness for late nights and deep sleepers.

The fallout from the gunfight still raged. Random shots, more numerous as the hours passed and the whiskey at the saloon flowed, punctuated darkness until the early hours of the morning. Word around town was that the shot killing Ernie was stray, intended for some unscrupulous horse thief. Tempers flared over the senseless act, making a few of Brown's Point more vocal citizens demand retribution. Whether or not anyone would ever be brought to justice for the act was doubtful but there was enough noise being made for a "necktie social" to keep everyone awake, even those who were safely in their beds.

The hullabaloo turned to Kristen's advantage. She took her time perusing the available goods. The items on display were shoddy by comparison to the finer pieces she would have been able to purchase back home but there was no helping it; these goods would have to do.

"I'd like six skeins of blue embroidery thread. The same number of wide-eyed needles, please. And six of those lace-trimmed linen hankies, if you will." She pointed to her selections, and watched the clerk remove the items from the display case. When the small pile was placed on the counter before her, she nodded her approval. "Perfect, thank you."

"Will there be anything else, ma'am?"

"No, this will do." She reached into the buttoned wrist of her left glove and pulled out a small wad of cash. It was intentionally kept separate from her own funds; she didn't want to chance confusing the girls' money with her own. If there was any change due them, they would be sure to get it. Kristen paid the man, and then slid the extra bill back into her glove. The coins she dropped into the paper sack with the embroidery supplies. "Have a nice day."

"You too. And come again, please."

She acknowledged his invitation with a smile and fast nod before she took a step back from the sales counter.

"You're up early."

Jack's observance, as well as his presence, caught her off guard. She jumped, visibly startled.

"Whoa there, calm down," he said, reaching a steadying hand out and placing it on her shoulder. "I didn't mean to give you such a fright. I'm sorry."

She shook away his apology with a wave of her hand. "You didn't frighten me, so there's no need to apologize. I just didn't expect to see you behind me, that's all. It seems like you and I are destined to bump into each other, doesn't it?"

Jack pulled his hand back, and stuck it casually in his pocket. She noticed he carried a rifle in his other hand. It was the first time she had seen it, so its presence caught her attention. Her gaze fixed on the weapon's long barrel. It was polished to a high shine, and she wondered how much effort it took to keep it so pristine. The stock, a dark wood, looked equally well cared for. Jack's hand fit around its widest part with room to spare. She had never taken such notice of Jack's hands before and hadn't realized they were so large. While the weapon appeared heavy, he carried it with apparent ease. The man and rifle were a good fit for each other.

He chuckled, the deep gravelly sound of his voice sending a lightning-fast shiver up Kristen's spine. She smiled, and hoped she didn't look as wobbly as she felt.

Just being in Jack's presence brought a whole new level of pleasure to the morning. His appearance also did peculiar things to her stomach. Perhaps she should have postponed the shopping trip until after breakfast. A full stomach might have eliminated the unsteady feeling sweeping over her.

"It does, doesn't it? Still, I should have announced my presence, or at least cleared my throat." He paused, looking deeply into her eyes.

Had someone else gazed at her this way, Kristen would have felt like a bug on the end of a child's fingertip, open to scrutiny and having its antennae and legs counted. But Jack didn't make her feel like he pried where he shouldn't, or that his gaze was anything less than proper. His assessment was as gentle as a soft, warm breeze blowing off the ocean, and she felt in the brief moment that she was back at home and standing on the beach facing the open Atlantic.

"I have to admit, I was enjoying the pleasure of observing you."

The unexpected flattery brought heat to her cheeks.

"Whatever do you mean?"

He shrugged, the nonchalant gesture bringing his shirtfront tight over his shoulder muscles. "That's self-explanatory, isn't it? You were so engrossed—so charmingly engrossed—in selecting your sewing supplies that I became...well, I suppose I became engrossed in watching you. By the way, what exactly are you sewing? It looks like you've got enough thread and whatnot to stitch a whole ships' sail. Is that what you're planning? To build a ship and sail it out of here, its mast hung with a blue-hemmed sail?"

The joke made Kristen laugh. *A ship! In this land-locked frontier?*

"Oh, yes, now you've discovered my secret." They began to walk toward the front of the store. A woman with a pair of squabbling children had entered, and the serenity of the shop had vanished. By mutual unspoken agreement they headed for the exit. "A ship, that's what I'm sewing up. And it's going to be one dandy of a vessel, too!"

"I knew you were a woman of many mysterious talents, but I had no idea ship-building was in your vast repertoire." He stood aside, holding the door wide. They stepped out onto the walkway, leaving the noisy children behind.

The day was beginning to warm up, and the sun was still far from high in the sky. It was going to be another scorcher. A ship sounded less silly and more like wishful thinking as they walked slowly along the wooden sidewalk.

"Mysterious? Is that what you think I am?" Back home she might have eschewed the question, not wishing to be thought coy, but here it felt natural to speak one's mind—to a point.

Jack slung the rifle over his left shoulder. He crooked his other elbow and offered it to her. Kristen's hand slipped into the space provided like it was meant to be there.

"To be quite frank, yes. I can tell you're keeping a secret or two."

If you only knew.

Trying to appear casual, Kristen asked, "Oh? And how can you tell what I'm keeping hidden, Jack?"

He shook his head, chuckling again. "Oh, no, I didn't say I could tell what you're hiding, only that you are hiding something. And as for the how of it? I guess it comes with the territory. Business-wise, that is. In my line of work it pays to be able to size someone up, to take quick stock of their character and form a gut feeling about them. Instinct, I guess."

"I'm not trying to pry, but what line of work are you in?"

They reached the intersection of the town's two main streets. On one corner a rectangle of grassy scrub grew, encouraged to some semblance of green by the presence of an ancient cottonwood tree. The tree's branches formed a wide, sheltering canopy. Beneath the tree two benches provided a place to rest, or to watch passers-by. Jack nodded toward the spot. When Kristen nodded her agreement, they crossed the street and walked into the shade.

"Of course you're not prying. We're unraveling mysteries, aren't we? Anyhow, I'm a sawmill man. Actually the only mill in the county, so I get a fair chance to meet and greet, and do business with, all kinds of people."

"Have you worked in the mill for long?"

They sat side by side on one of the benches. Jack rested his rifle, its butt on the ground between his feet and the barrel pointing up into the tree branches. Kristen placed her sack of supplies on the bench by her side. They both rested their backs against the tree trunk. The air was marginally cooler.

"All my life." Jack removed his hat, setting it beside him. "My grandfather owned the mill. He built it when my father was a boy. My father should have taken his place when Grandfather died, but my parents were killed when I was a child so I inherited the place. Granddad knew it would come directly to me, so he brought me into the business when I was barely old enough to wear long pants. He taught me everything, and gave me a livelihood that I know and love. I owe him for that. I always will."

"Were you young when your parents were killed?"

Jack answered without hesitation. "I was. Very young, actually."

"Did your grandparents raise you?"

"They did. And I had one of the happiest childhoods ever. Now that Granddad is gone, Granny keeps me hopping but I can't say I mind. Much." He flashed a grin, and then went on. "She's a wonderful woman, and like I said, I owe them everything."

His admiration for the couple was apparent by the gleam in his eyes. Kristen was touched by his love, and admired the way he made no effort to conceal his feelings.

"Do you know you're the second man who's told me in as many days that he was raised by grandparents?"

Jack's brows knit. "Is that so?"

"Mmm hmm."

Now that the statement was out, there was no way to retrieve it. Had it been possible, Kristen would have recalled the observation, and swallowed the words down. Chalk it up to Aunt Irene's intuition, but somehow she knew without being told that Jack didn't have a fond bone in his body where Patrick Godsend was concerned. He was never overtly rude to the other man, but it didn't take a Pony Express messenger to deliver the news that the pair barely tolerated each other.

She thought fast, hoping to turn the tide of the conversation, but Jack thought more quickly.

"Who?"

"Hmm?" Kristen swatted a slow hand at a mosquito buzzing near her ear.

Jack repeated the question. His voice had a sharpness to it she was unaccustomed to hearing. It annoyed her as much as the persistent mosquito but since swatting at Jack was out of the question, she answered him.

"Patrick Godsend. Pastor Godsend's grandson."

Even scowling, Jack looked handsome, and despite the displeasure dripping off his features, he was still, in an unaccountably unnerving sort of way, charming.

He rubbed his shoulders hard against the tree trunk, the rasping of his jacket on bark the only sound for a moment. The combination of his bear and man demeanor was almost impossible to ignore. Kristen grappled with herself; the impulse to throw her head back and laugh was strong.

Fortunately self-restraint won out over her sense of

humor.

"Humph! So his grandfather, the preacher, raised him?"

"That's right." Knowing bears crave honey more than anything else, Kristen attempted to placate him. "And that's probably the only thing the two of you have in common, isn't it?"

Her plan backfired. Jack's prickliness intensified, something she didn't expect and wasn't prepared to deal with.

"What's that supposed to mean?"

All desire to laugh fled, replaced by a tinge of indignation. He had no right to put her on the defensive, but that's what he had done.

"It doesn't mean anything, not really."

He wasn't the only one who could scowl—she pulled her brows together until her forehead hurt. Narrowing her eyes, she turned to face Jack.

"I just meant that you two don't seem alike, other than your upbringings. And even that's not really the same. Poor Patrick only had one grandparent to depend on."

"'Poor Patrick'! Why, it doesn't look to me like he's spent one minute of his life being poor—or suffering, either. No, those lily-white, never-touched-a-tool hands of his tell a completely different tale. Your 'Poor Patrick' is pampered, and probably spoiled, and hasn't so much as lifted one finger to do a hard, honest day's work in his whole life. Poor Patrick, my foot." Jack crossed his arms over his chest, lowered his chin and glowered.

The tantrum was more than Kristen wanted to deal with. Fleeing Boston had taught her a number of things, one of which was that she didn't have to put up with any man's guff. Let them have their fits, unreasonable demands and other eccentricities of the male gender. For all she cared, every man on earth could jump up and down, cross his eyes and toes or wave his fists in the air—and whether they did or didn't, she wasn't about to put up with their foolishness.

Kristen stood, grabbed her parcel and started out of the modest town park.

"Hey! Wait a minute! Where are you going?"

Jack's protest quickened her step. Keeping her back to him, she stepped out into the street. It was tough to hide her satisfaction, but she kept her amusement on her face and out of her voice.

"I've had enough of you for now, Jack Sterling," Kristen called airily over her shoulder. She worried he would follow, so she scooted into the path of a big black stallion and was relieved when its rider swerved around her. Raising her voice, and not caring one bit whether anyone heard her, she added, "You're behaving like a spoiled little boy. I don't have the patience for such nonsense. Good day!"

Chapter Ten

Had it been physically possible to do so, Jack would have put his own boot print on his backside. How could he have been so stupid?

He had ruined what promised to be a cozy moment with the first woman to stir his romantic interests in longer than… Good God in heaven, in longer than he could remember! Even when he wracked his brain, searching for the memory of another female who stirred him the way Kristen did, he came up blank. Perfectly blank, not even the slightest glimmer of recognition for anyone else who had ignited his undeniably finicky interest.

There was no accounting for it. He must be out of his cotton-picking, ever-loving mind. Any other excuse for his outrageous behavior was just that, an excuse. No, he had to be crazy. What else could it be?

Granddad would have an explanation for this temporary insanity of mine.

He huffed, exasperated, annoyed and just plain puzzled by his actions. Back home, he was completely in control at all times. But here? And with Miss Kristen Marsh? Why, he could barely keep a civil tongue. What a fool he had made of himself.

She was enough to drive every ounce of common sense right out of his head. No, that wasn't the whole unvarnished truth. It wasn't so much the lady that drove him nuts—although she certainly had a way about her that strongly affected him. No, it was the thought of Kristen doing anything—even talking—with that softheaded Patrick Godsend.

There was no rational excuse he could give her for his foolish behavior.

And there was no way he could simply ignore the fact that he'd acted like an escapee from a mental institution.

No, he'd have to clear the air when he next saw Kristen.

So, a gift of some sort…preferably the frivolous-but-pretty variety favored by so many women. He knew exactly what to get.

Fortunately the shop was, once again, deserted. The morning bustle was over and the afternoon shoppers had not yet arrived. Jack walked right to the counter, his boots beating out a rhythm that matched the pounding in his chest.

Good God in Heaven, what if she decides not to speak to me again? I acted like a jealous colt, with less brains that brawn and probably laced up her view that men who aren't from Boston—or the pulpit—are untamed.

A fresh wave of embarrassment hit him. Jack slapped his palm against the wooden countertop. The sting was but a small atonement, and he knew it.

The clerk's glance shot from Jack's hand to his face. Apparently he felt no threat, because he stepped closer. His pasty complexion made Jack want to shoo the young man outside, into the warmth of the day. He looked unwell.

"What can I do for you? And weren't you in here

earlier? This morning, with a pretty lady—yes, I'm sure it was you." His welcoming smile stretched. "Of course, I never forget a face."

"Never?"

"Nope. Never. Well, almost never, leastways." Planting his hands on the counter, and leaning closer still, he asked, "So? What'll it be?" He swept a glance from Jack's hat to his boot tips. "We got a little bit of everything. Spurs, hats, denim workpants if the ones you've got are your only pair. Socks, though during these hot months there ain't much call for the woolen ones but we got those too, if you've a mind for some. Let's see…we got a fair selection of mining tools, although I got to admit Jake over at the Smithy has got some mighty fine hand-hammered items. Now, what else…?"

Jack held a hand up to stop him. "I already know what I need."

The clerk scratched behind his right ear with an index finger that looked like it hadn't seen a bar of lye soap in a month of Sundays.

"Well why didn't you say so, then? You could've saved a feller the trouble of ticking off the display shelves if you'd let on you know what you need."

"Ah, I didn't mean to let you go on so. It was…" Jack shrugged diplomatically. "It was just interesting to hear that you offer such a vast array of goods. And in such a compact space, too. Why, you've got a real knack for showing the stock to its best advantage."

Annoyance turned instantly to pride.

"Why, we do have a real nice place here, don't we? My missus and me, we bought it from her papa. Well, we own the building but the bank gave us the seed money to stock up and all. That Mr. Brown, he's a good man. If it wasn't for his generosity you wouldn't see so many fancy things in these here showcases. No sir, we wouldn't have been able to keep such a fine place if it wasn't for Brown's Bank."

Brown. Everywhere he turned he either ran headfirst into that crook Randall Brown or the preacher's grandson. Would he have no rest until he shook the dust of this town off his boot heels?

Jack ignored the reference to the banker. He pointed to the front window's display ledge.

"There is a pair of ear bobs in the front window. Silver with turquoise inlay. I'll take them."

****

Kristen pulled herself back to reality.

Daydreams were nice, but in their proper time and place. With barely an hour to prepare for the first lesson, this was neither.

It still hadn't sunk in that the germ of the idea, planted so innocently over the previous night's mashed potatoes and chicken, had grown so quickly. By the time the earliest rays of sunshine swept across her brow through the lacy curtains, Kristen had lain awake beneath the counterpane nearly all night debating whether she'd had a brilliant idea or merely a wishful dream.

But she hadn't been dreaming. One innocent, wistful remark had been enough to set her on a new path. She would have to think of something special to do for Julia, especially if this plan was a success.

Over slices of delectable peach pie, she had broached the subject of giving private elocution lessons to her fellow boarders. The idea had been so enthusiastically received that the first lesson was set to take place this very afternoon.

It was almost too much for Kristen to believe, that she could be paid to teach the basic rules and practices of gentility. She had taken so many of her talents for granted, the lessons for each having begun so early in her life that the ins and outs of needlework, languages, social graces, watercolors and a plethora of likewise information seemed ingrained, part and parcel of who and what she was.

Fortunately for her, not every woman had received the same education. Julia, Geraldine, Roberta, Justine and Eliza were anxious to broaden their horizons. Only Edith had refused the offer of lessons. She wasn't as warm toward Kristen as the other women, so it wasn't surprising when she claimed to have other things to better occupy her time. Her disdain at the proposal hadn't thwarted anyone's enthusiasm. Besides, five pupils were more than enough to keep Kristen's mind—and hands—busy.

Hopefully her purse would benefit from the arrangement. The initial lessons offered were thrice-weekly afternoon embroidery sessions and hour-long, post-dinner meetings to discuss etiquette. Those, also, were tentatively scheduled to take place three times a week. All had agreed upon a modest fee, and each woman agreed to pay Kristen at the end of each week for the number of lessons attended. To keep track, Kristen drew up a basic ledger page, listing five pupils and leaving room to fill in which classes they attended.

Mrs. King, the boardinghouse owner, had heard the plan and confessed she had once been part of eastern society. A husband with a mining urge had brought her out west. When he passed on, she had stayed but said she still missed more genteel pursuits. With unbridled enthusiasm, Mrs. King had even volunteered to step in and teach any class if Kristen found herself one day otherwise occupied.

The arrangement looked, on the surface, perfect. However, a troublesome finger of doubt had poked Kristen all day long. What if the lessons proved to be a disaster? What then? She had no other method of support figured out, so without the lessons she would be back where she started. Worse off, even. When she began her journey she had at least had a small nest egg. Now she was practically destitute.

This has to work. Nothing can go wrong. Nothing.

"Kristen?" Julia drew the last syllable out in a singsong fashion. "You've got a visitor at the front door. Should I let the feller—ah, the *gentleman*—in or would you like to take his call on the porch? I don't mind relaying a message, if you've a mind to give one. It ain't any trouble at all."

She let the slip slide, especially since it was obvious Julia had attempted some measure of gentility in her announcement of the unexpected caller. Had this been Boston, there would have been a calling card. But, as she reminded herself at least a dozen times each day, this wasn't Boston.

Kristen threw her hands up in frustration. If she accepted a caller, who would finish setting up the chairs? She had only pulled half of them into a circle in the parlor.

Julia quickly offered to help. "You're getting the chairs together here, ain't you? Why don't you let me finish, so you can go see the man outside."

"You don't mind?" Refusal was out of the question. "The last two are over there." She pointed to a pair of blue side chairs.

"I don't mind at all. Go on, see the guy. He's mighty cute, if I do say so myself. And, he's got that look on his face."

Halfway to the parlor door, Kristen stopped. *That look?*

"What do you mean? What kind of look is on his face?"

Julia was in the process of dragging one of the chairs across the worn rug. Julia crossed to the first blue chair and tugged it over the rug, talking over her shoulder while she worked. "Oh, you know the look I mean. It's the kind that says he's done something wrong, and he knows it. More to the point, he knows you know he's been a creep. If I was the wagering kind—and I'm not, mind you—but if I was, I'd bet my bottom dollar he's here to beg forgiveness."

With a soft grunt and the push of one hip, Julia moved the chair into position. She wiped her palms down the sides of her dress, looked up at Kristen and asked, "So, what did the feller do? And are you going to forgive him for it or not? Me? I'd let him wiggle like a worm on a hook for a spell before I caved in, but that's just me. You do what you want. After all, you're the teacher and I'm just the pupil."

Julia's grin was lost on Kristen. She suspected her apprentice had much more experience with men, fish and hooks than she did. Was it possible the wrong person was giving lessons here?

Julia was right. The man on the porch was handsome, sorrowful-looking and, as he turned to face

Kristen when she came outside, looking to make amends. Patrick's expression, coupled with the way he worried his hat's brim between his fists, was all but comical.

Had she not been concerned an immediate pardon might give the wrong impression, or lead to a second round of amorous advances, she might have laughed aloud. Instead, Kristen concentrated on staying solemn in the face of his discomfort. It was tough, but she managed to keep a bland expression.

"Whatever are you doing here? I thought we concluded our…ah, our dealings for the day." Her tone was deliberately neutral. Mindful of the hour and her first lesson, she added, "I'm on a schedule, so please get to your point."

"I don't blame you for being angry with me."

He closed the space between them with one large step, forcing Kristen to bend her neck backward and look up at him. Concern tugged his brows together, and once again she had to try to contain her amusement. Patrick must have seen the flicker of emotion in her eyes, however, because his lips twitched, chasing some of the seriousness from his face.

"Dare I hope? Maybe you're not as angry as I think you are, then?"

She took a step back, bringing her spine in contact with the closed door. The movement didn't put much extra space between them physically but she hoped it might convey an unspoken message.

"No, you're right. I am annoyed with you." *And nearly every other man in town, practically.* "Your behavior by the creek was shocking. I thought better of you, Patrick. Really, I did, and I'm disappointed that you did…that you tried…ah, that you acted in such—well, you know what you did. I don't need to explain."

He studied her silently. His hands had stopped crushing his hat brim. Now, he turned and placed the hat on a small wooden table beside the door. Then he stepped a few inches closer, all the while looking deeply into Kristen's eyes.

She reached a hand behind her and found the doorknob. The knowledge that escape was but a fast turn of the wrist away steadied her galloping insides. She lifted her chin, the defiant pose one she had learned at her father's knee. Sometimes it worked to get her what she wanted. Other times it didn't, but it might just add some credence to her side of the debate.

"Are you so angry that you won't forgive me? Were my actions so despicable that they are unpardonable?"

Patrick swept a fingertip across her cheek. She would have twisted away had he not pushed an errant lock of hair up toward her right ear. She reached a shaking finger to finish tucking the stray curl into place.

"What's it to be, Kristen my sweet? Will you forgive me or not?"

"Don't call me that," she whispered. Endearments were meant to be reserved for lovers. She and Patrick would never, ever be that close. They would never be lovers. The sound brought heat to her face, but a chill to her heart. "It's not right, and you know it."

"You haven't answered my question." He held her gaze captive with his. She felt exposed and vulnerable to his scrutiny. "Will you forgive me? You know in your heart it's the right thing to do, to forgive someone their misdemeanors. Say you'll forgive me."

"I will. But don't do…ah…" She hated being trapped. Her hand tightened its grip on the doorknob but, despite the lure it dangled before her, she stubbornly refused to turn it. She cleared her throat and chased the tremor from her voice. "Don't do what you did down by the creek again, Patrick. I mean it."

He heaved a sigh, and then nodded. "Thank you for your pardon. I appreciate your kindness regarding my indiscreet behavior." His eyes searched hers for so long she wanted to look away.

With an expression not much changed from the one he'd worn when she first opened the door and stepped onto the porch, Patrick nodded a second time.

"Fine. I'll honor your wishes but I've got to say— even if it's just once that I say it—that I'm attracted to you, Kristen. I may be a preacher's grandson, and a man with some hard and heavy ties to scripture, but I'm still a man. And a man has feelings and—no, I see your eyes growing round at my words and I don't want to rile you again so I'll stop here but you know now how I feel." He took his hat from the table and fitted it on his head. With a sweet, yet regretful, smile, Patrick said, "I just want you to know that while I fancy you, I won't wait forever for you to return my feelings. A man's got to find companionship, and build a family, so I want to be clear that if you don't indicate you might have some romantic leanings my way, I'll move my sights elsewhere."

His honesty loosened the knots in Kristen's stomach, as well as her grip on the doorknob at her back. She brought her hands together at her waist and jerked her head in understanding. "I understand."

Patrick leaned close, his breath warm against her

cheek as he spoke directly into her right ear. "I do hope you'll change your mind. Really, I do."

Chapter Eleven

Things weren't going the way he planned. By now the deed should be safely back in his saddlebag. He should be halfway home to Kansas. And the last thing on Jack's mind should be a woman—even if she was by far the most beautiful, honey-haired woman he'd ever run across.

With those deeper-than-deep blue eyes...he couldn't forget those eyes. Every time he closed his own, Kristen's cerulean blues haunted his dreams.

Why hadn't he just ridden by when he saw that stagecoach being robbed? He could have waited for a more opportune time to reclaim his deed. There might have been a moment before it found its way into Randall Brown's greasy fingers when he might have snatched it back, tucked it into his coat pocket and turned his horse, Midnight, around. If he'd done that, taken a more sensible approach to the matter, Kansas soil would be beneath his feet now instead of the red powder that passed for ground in this Godforsaken wilderness.

Why didn't I leave that stagecoach alone? What was I thinking, throwing myself on top of that woman?

Jack slapped a hand across his thigh, the stinging on his palm strangely satisfying. It reminded him that although his mind was in turmoil his body was, as ever it was, in full control. That, at least, was something.

He walked down the street at a slow pace, with no reason to hurry. He had nowhere to go.

A bee in my bonnet. That's what Granny would say is troubling me.

The previous afternoon he witnessed that preacher's grandson keeping company with Kristen on the front porch of the boardinghouse. Jack was glad he hadn't rushed right over, demanded an explanation and, once again, left his breeding and manners in the dust. No, he'd leaned against a tree, the shade of its slender branches effectively hiding him from view. He had seen the entire exchange, and even though he hadn't been able to hear a word, he got a pretty clear indication of what happened.

Jack shook his head, a grin crossing his face. The warm glow of satisfaction built inside him, and he chuckled.

It's just too bad, isn't it, that "Poor Patrick" got the boot. A crying shame…

They both wanted the same thing, and only one man could get the prize.

Why should he feel sorry for the other man? Even a child could tell after seeing yesterday's exchange that Kristen wasn't attracted to him. Oh, sure, it was possible she was playing some kind of cat-and-mouse game, but Jack didn't think it was the case. It didn't seem likely that a woman with as much intelligence as Kristen would stoop to taking part in nonsensical romantic amusements.

The Battle of Beecher's Island, back in the fall of '68, hadn't felt this strategic. Back then, he'd taken orders and done his best with them. When Colonel Forsyth said to take his Spencer Carbine and advance, he'd made certain he had nine shots in the rifle and moved forward with the rest of his contingent.

There had been a plan, of sorts, and a clear-cut view of the enemy. Hundreds of Cheyenne and Sioux warriors had stormed them, but they'd held their ground and won the battle. It had been no stretch of the imagination, knowing what to do and when to act. Instinct had been his best friend, his gut the compass by which he found direction. His rifle had saved his life. His wits had kept him alive until reinforcements arrived on the tiny spit of land. And his instinct had been to never, ever put himself in such peril again—not if he wanted to live to see old age.

Since meeting Kristen, he'd broken his own rule more than once. If he wasn't putting himself between her and danger, he was contemplating doing so. And if he wasn't thinking about her, he was consumed by yearning for the sight, sound—even the lavender scent—of her.

Jack had fallen hard for the sweet vixen, and he hated himself for it.

Theirs was a relationship doomed to failure before it even got its start. He knew that, but still his heart ignored logic.

Maybe it would be better to hand Kristen the ear bobs, thank her for her friendship and then just walk away from her. The coward's way out, but his heart, and probably his dignity, might remain intact.

Who was he trying to kid? Kristen Marsh hadn't even forgiven him for his childish behavior, and here he pondered how best to rid himself of his affliction for her?

Jack huffed a disgusted breath. Thank God, no one

could read his mind.

Pulling himself from the trappings of his subconscious, he lengthened his stride. He had no idea where he was headed, but maybe if he walked with some sense of purpose his woman-softened brain might stop venturing into the realm of ridiculousness.

Then again, he might, with purpose, mind, walk right on over to that boardinghouse and see what Miss Kristen Marsh had planned for this afternoon.

Jack turned on his boot heel and switched directions. The idea of an afternoon stroll with Kristen appealed to him. He was, after all, human. And a man.

"Kristen, do you mind helping me just a mite with this stitching? I've been at it like a hound dog on a soup bone but I just ain't—ah, aren't?—" Julia sucked her lower lip between her teeth. She frowned, obviously at a loss.

So far she had only given one elocution and grammar lesson, but its effect was apparent.

"'I'm not having success'..." she prompted.

Julia stopped worrying her lip, and smiled. "That's it! I'm not having no success—"

Kristen interrupted gently. "*Any* success."

"Oh, right. I'm not having any success with this here...ah, with this stitching." She held her embroidery hoop out. Threads dangled from the fabric, waving like kite tails in a soft breeze. "See?"

Smiling, Kristen took the handwork. If the hanging threads were any hint at the condition of the sampler, it was going to take more than a "mite" of assistance to untangle!

Julia had completely missed the idea of creating tiny, almost hidden, knots to secure her stitches. The piece in the hoop was riddled with clumsy knots, uneven stitching and, when she turned it over to examine the backside, Kristen saw the thread dragged over large patches of bare fabric.

Julia reached out, as if to snatch the offensive piece of fabric back, but Kristen kept a firm grip on the hoop. She put her arm down by her side, and hid the handwork in the folds of her navy blue skirt.

She took a deep, cleansing breath and put one arm around her pupil's shoulders. "We can fix this. There are a couple of steps I may not have been clear enough on, so I'm going to clarify a few things for you. Then, we will remove some of your stitches and I'll show you how to redo them. I'm sure you'll have the techniques down in no time."

"Do you really think so?"

"I do," she replied with more conviction than she felt. The hoop felt heavy in her hand, a scrap of fabric filled with examples of all the things she had said not to do. If Kristen had wanted to create a hands-on rendering of just what she hoped her pupils would avoid, it would look exactly like the piece she held.

"I feel like I'm all thumbs with a needle and thread," Julia confessed. She held out her right thumb for inspection. It was pinpricked all over, with tiny scabs on the top of some of the marks. The woman had bled over her handwork.

Kristen recognized the look of the thumb, having seen it on other handwork pupils. She had never struggled with stitching when she had been learning, at an age far younger than Julia's, but she remembered other girls whose thumbs bore scars from the sharp tip of a stitching needle.

"There's no shame in having difficulty learning a new craft, Julia. In fact, I love it that you're asking for some extra help."

"I'm willing to pay you for this," Julia said quickly. "I don't want you to work for nothing."

"You mean, 'Work without compensation.'"

"Right—without compensation." When Julia smiled, her dimples showed. "Compensation sounds fancier than nothing, doesn't it? Anyway, like I was saying, I don't want you to think I want this special attention for—without compensating you. I don't make it my business to dance for free, and that's an awful lot easier to do than this stitching, so I sure don't expect you to teach me on the side for—oh, without compensation."

"I understand. But I don't mind helping unravel your stitching, and the compensation will be watching you master the stitches. Now, let's get to it."

Leading Julia toward the empty parlor, Kristen put the thought of the walk she had been hoping to take out of her mind. For the next hour or so, Julia and her embroidery should take priority over her own wishes. Maybe afterward, though, there might still be time for a short stroll. She hoped so; there was someone she looked forward to—if she was fortunate—"accidentally" bumping into. It had happened before, it might happen again!

But first, Julia's embroidery.

Chapter Twelve

"You're just the man I was looking for."

As much as Jack wanted his family's deed back, and to quickly conclude his business with Brown, he wished the man hadn't found what he was looking for. Leastways, not at this precise moment. Couldn't the land grabber have waited for a better time?

Slowly, Jack turned toward the bank where Brown stood smiling from the front step.

"Is that so?" He took his time walking back to Brown. The banker must have seen Jack pass, probably through the glass window in his office, and come after him.

You weren't here when I came by a second ago. Must've crawled out from under your rock and into the sunshine.

His granny would have smacked him had she been privy to his unkind thoughts. But she wasn't, so he was free to think what he wanted, when he wanted to think it. And now, dislike as thick as tar covered his feelings—and thoughts—regarding the frontier banker.

"It is." Brown wore no overcoat, and his shirtsleeves were rolled up. The tanned forearms and wrists once again seemed out of place. How could a man so obviously accustomed to being outdoors stand to be cooped inside a musty old bank all day long? No amount of money could entice Jack to the job—

101

especially when it involved swindling honest people.

He reminded himself why he had come to this middle-of-nowhere town. Randall Brown was a crook—and it irked Jack that the land thief stood smiling smugly down at him.

They couldn't talk this way, not out in the open on the street like a pair of gunslingers. And standing ten inches lower than his opponent was out of the question.

Jack nodded toward the bank's empty lot.

"How about we discuss matters beneath that..." He cast a dubious eye on the scraggly, forlorn elm tree. "...ah, that sorry little tree? I think it might throw enough shade for us to both stand out of the sun. Then again, maybe not."

Without waiting to see if he was being followed, Jack walked to the tree. He removed his hat, ran his fingers through his damp curls, then placed the Stetson firmly back onto his head. If he had been back at his office at the mill, and about to begin a business conversation, he would have straightened his tie and shot his sleeves inside his jacket. But here, adjusting his hair and hat was as good as it got.

When he was done, he turned. Randall Brown stood right behind him. They were close but there was no help for it. The canopy of sun-scorched leaves was barely big enough for one man. Two was a squeeze.

A pulse throbbed in the banker's temple.

Jack wondered if his adversary was excited—or nervous, perhaps? He hoped it was a combination of both. Nervous excitement sometimes threw men off, and gave their opponents the upper hand. Jack never minded having the upper hand—in any game, particularly one where the stakes were so high.

"Well?" Jack knew his attitude was surly but he didn't care. A man who stole from widows and honest families didn't deserve courtesy. "What drew you out of your—" He stopped himself before he said "hole". Taking a deep breath, he finished, "office?"

"I told you, I wanted to see you." Brown rocked back on his heels. His spurs dug crescent-shaped depressions in the dust behind his feet. He shrugged. "When I saw you walk by, I figured it's as good a time as any to have a word. It's not as if I hunted you down with a posse, Sterling. You were in plain sight, you know."

"So I was."

Although the other man's words were genial, without even the slightest undertone of malice, Jack still didn't trust him. How could he? Somewhere inside that bank building, in the vault most likely, hid the deed to his Kansas home. Even with Brown acting chummy, there was no way in heaven or…well, there was just no way at all he was going to let his guard drop.

He'd have sooner turned his back on a hungry black bear than on a smiling banker. It was another of his grandfather's lessons he'd learned early; trust those who seem to be seeking approval the hardest the least. They were the ones, Granddad had admonished, who most often had an ulterior motive.

"Now that you've waylaid me, what's on your mind?"

Brown chuckled. He didn't wear a hat, so his eyes were unshaded and, as such, it was clear how much he was amused by Jack's manner.

Amusement? It was nearly an insult. The hair on the nape of Jack's neck rose, and his trigger finger formed a curl around his holster fastening. He'd killed men for less during the War. Who was he kidding? During the War he had killed because he'd been ordered to do so, or he had feared for his own life or the lives of innocent people. But wartime was over, and in this day of reason and somewhat peaceful times, any man could show amusement without having his head blown off.

Jack relaxed his hand, and in particular his finger. He grit his teeth and waited for the other man's answer.

A mule brayed in the distance. Further off, the sound of a train whistle, mournful against the mundane sounds of Main Street.

"When we last spoke, you promised you would get what was rightfully yours back. Now, I don't ever mind a man keeping what's his. Why, it's the American way, don't you think? We all work hard for what we've got. We've got a right to keep what's rightfully ours. Don't you agree?"

Disagreeing would have been ridiculous. Jack agreed with every word out of Brown's mouth—so far—so he nodded.

"I thought you might be a reasonable man."

"I'm reasonable all right. Reasonable enough to want what's mine returned to me."

The banker paused. He and Jack locked gazes, standing so still and silent they looked carved of stone.

"I can understand that." Brown shrugged, as if the matter was settled. "But I don't see how that concerns me. Not one bit."

"You've got the deed to my family's place. I want it back." A muscle worked in Jack's jaw. His teeth closed tightly around every word as he fought the anger swirling within him. "I mean to get it, one way or another. You've got something that's mine, and I have no intention of letting you keep it."

"Well, that's where you and I take different forks in the road, I'm afraid. I don't believe I've got anything that belongs to you, or your family."

Jack swallowed hard. Bile rose in his throat.

It took a hard man to steal, and then smile at the person he had stolen from.

"You're denying you've got the Carroll Junction deed to the Sterling homestead? Is that what you're saying?"

Randall Brown shook his head, but he didn't look away. He stared into Jack's eyes and said, "I don't deny that I do. In fact, I checked and I've got the Sterling deed, as well as several others. All located in and around Carroll's Junction, Kansas."

The audacity of the man! "You admit it, then?"

"Of course I do. Why shouldn't I admit I've got them? They are, after all, mine."

Jack's left hand curled into a fist but he kept it tight against his thigh. The impulse to slug the banker on the chin made him see red, but not so red that he couldn't at least give the man one more chance to come clean.

"Those deeds are no more yours than this beetle-infested tree is mine!" He slapped the tree trunk so hard the tree shook.

"Hey, watch that tree! My grandfather planted it when he founded Brown's Point. I admit, it's taken a while for it to grow but it's a long way from Kansas." He placed his hand on the tree trunk, then leaned his weight so he and the tree stood as one. "Transplants take time, Sterling. It might be stupid to some, but my family's roots—and their transplants—mean a great deal to me. A very great deal. I'd appreciate it if you kept that in mind."

Had he heard right? Was the Brown family from Kansas, too?

"Your grandfather brought the tree from Kansas?"

Brown nodded. "He did. Planted it with his own hands, said it was going to take root in this red dirt if he had to spoon-feed it himself to make it grow. My grandfather's long gone, but the tree, and the town he founded, remain. My heritage means a lot to me, and I'll expect you to respect that."

"As does mine," Jack countered. "And if you respected my heritage, I'd respect yours. But you haven't bought the deed to my family's home—you've stolen it. There's no way I can leave this place without it. The way I see it, you can just hand it over and, being a Christian and not wanting unnecessary bloodshed, I'm willing to walk away. God knows, I've seen enough blood in my days to last a lifetime."

His days of fighting Indians were behind him. He never wanted to take another man's life, or harm him in any way, if he could help it.

"That's mighty generous of you, Sterling, to offer not to fill my hide with shots. I appreciate the gesture, really I do, but the fact remains I have no intention of handing over what rightfully belongs to me." Brown stared into Jack's eyes, and Jack saw the same determination coursing through his veins reflected back at him from the depths of the other man's eyes.

It was a stalemate, and they both saw it.

"It's mine, I tell you." Jack waved a fist in the air between them.

"And I tell you, the Kansas property is mine. Bought and paid for, and all mine," Brown insisted.

"We'll just see about that."

"I guess we will, although I don't see how you can say the place still belongs to you when, for starters, I've got the deed in my wall safe." Brown lifted his shoulders, then let them drop, the motion so slow and deliberate it was an unspoken challenge.

Jack never turned from a challenge. He wasn't about to start to do so now.

"The *stolen* deed."

"I paid for that property, just like I did for all the rest of the Kansas properties I bought. I would think you'd be here to thank me, instead of to call me a liar and a thief. Really, Sterling, you should be shaking my hand and expressing bottomless gratitude."

"You must stay out in the sun too long without your hat," Jack sneered. "Why in blazes would I thank you for stealing my property?"

The banker shook his head, as if the whole conversation taxed him. "I keep telling you, I didn't *steal* anything. Never have, never will. And frankly I'm getting tired of you saying that I am a thief. I've given you leeway on the point up until now but I don't want to hear the insinuation again. Do you understand?"

Jack opened his mouth to speak, and would have called the other man a liar and a thief yet again but Brown held up a hand and went on.

"I paid good money for that property—real good money. Like I said, you should be thanking me for being so generous. I didn't have to be, you know. But, as I keep telling you, I don't make it my business to steal from anyone, so I was more than fair with the price offered on each and every one of those Kansas properties. And I can prove it." Brown crossed his arms over his chest and leaned back against the tree trunk. A bead of perspiration slid down one cheek but that was the only indication he gave that he was in any way bothered by the heat.

Would be hard for a crook to look so cool under pressure.

"You say you can prove you 'bought' my place?"

Brown nodded. A self-satisfied smile played around the edges of his lips. "I can."

"How?"

"The receipts for every purchase are in my safe, along with the deeds. I can prove I bought them all fair and square, and show how much I paid for them."

The world tilted beneath his boot heels. Was it possible that there was a bill of sale for Granny's place? And if there was, and the place had legitimately sold, where was the money?

More importantly—by far—were the questions flying through his mind faster than a runaway stallion. Was Granny Sterling losing her mind? Surely she couldn't have forgotten she had sold the place...could she?

Chapter Thirteen

"Look! I did it! No one can say that this here ain't—uh, *isn't*—one beautiful French knot, can they, Kristen?" Geraldine, clad in a rose-colored wrap that matched her skin tone perfectly, looked up in triumph. Six or seven inches of embroidery thread—rose-colored, as well—hung from her lower lip. She carelessly blew it away, and held up her handiwork for the other women to inspect.

Kristen reached over, took the woman's hoop from her hand and examined the pink knot. It was firm and tight, and close to the fabric without pulling the weave unevenly. The knot, one of the most difficult stitches to master, looked like it had been done by a professional.

She raised one eyebrow. "It is a perfect French knot. Geraldine, are you sure you've never worked a needle before? This doesn't look like a beginner's knot—not by any stretch of the imagination."

Kristen handed the hoop back. The dancer had already begun to rethread her needle, this time with sky-blue floss, and seemed anxious to get her fingers working again.

When she had poked the needle into the fabric, Geraldine looked up and said, "Oh, I didn't say I'd never worked a needle before, remember? I said I never tried any of this fancy stitchin' you're teaching us, that's all. But, land sakes, I sure enough have held a needle more than I care to confess." She held up the tiny silver sewing needle before her eyes, examined it, and then smiled broadly. With a shake of her curls, she stuck it back into her fabric and said, "But I never did see a needle this puny. No, never."

Puny? The needle? It was a standard embroidery size. In fact, the needles Kristen had chosen for the beginners' class had larger-than-customary eyes, so that they would be easier for unfamiliar fingers to hold.

Kristen sighed. She had never meant for the afternoon to drag on the way it had, with her being stuck indoors on such a beautiful day. But once she and Julia straightened out the mess in Julia's hoop, Geraldine had woken and stuck her head in the parlor. Delight at the unexpected sewing lesson had made her dash upstairs for her embroidery. What had been a one-on-one session had turned into a full-blown sewing circle. Kristen saw no polite way to extricate herself from the affair.

"Just what kind of needle are you more familiar with?" Kristen patiently asked.

Grinning, Geraldine looked up from her needlework. She already had a row of blue French knots surrounding the first rose colored one, and Kristen saw the beginning of a free-style flower taking shape. The woman's creativity was admirable, as was her ability to pick up embroidery so quickly.

"Why, the kind farmers use on livestock, of course! My daddy is a Mississippi farmer, remember? And since he and Momma only had girls, we all farmed right along with him. So I ain't no stranger to a livestock needle, but that's the only kind I ever held before this one. And, you've got to believe me when I say a livestock needle puts this little feller to shame."

There were many things in life that aroused Kristen's curiosity. Livestock needles? That was a question that was much, much better left unasked.

I don't want to know…

Just as Kristen got a mind picture of what she thought a livestock needle might look like, Julia changed the subject. Thank goodness!

"There's a new preacher in town. Hear tell he's planning to start up Sunday services again over at the church."

Kristen looked over at her friend, but Julia kept her head bent low over her embroidery.

"I came in on the same stage as Pastor Godsend. He's a gentleman, and was excellent company on the long ride." She leaned across the arm of her chair, and then smiled in satisfaction at the enchanting clusters of "petals" taking shape on Geraldine's flower. She sat back, resting against her chair and watched the two women at their sewing. They had taken to the skill like ducks to water, and it did Kristen's heart good to feel her presence in some small way impacted life in this rugged town. She went on, "He is, of course, incredibly knowledgeable about Scripture, but he's got a number of other intriguing interests as well. We spoke at length about all sorts of things…"

"Ain't he—uh, doesn't he have a grandson?" Julia asked.

Geraldine's curls bounced against her shoulders as she spun around and beamed a smile at Kristen. "A baby! How sweet! Why, you must have had a whole lot of fun taking turns holding the little feller, and bouncing him on your lap, cuddling him close and watching him sleep. Oh, I just love babies…Mamma always had a young one for us to coddle. I miss that, you know. Not many babies out here, not that I come in contact with, leastways."

Julia stopped embroidering. She stuck her needle into the corner edge of her fabric, dropped the hoop onto her lap and sat back. Waving her hand before her reddened face, she said, "Mercy, it's hot in here."

No reply seemed in order, so Kristen just smiled. Geraldine was engrossed in her sewing and didn't even look up from her fabric.

Julia had something on her mind, and wasted no time getting to the point.

"The preacher's grandson isn't a babe, is he?"

"No, he's not."

"He was—no, he is that handsome feller who came calling on you, isn't he?" Julia's fingers tightened on the arms of her chair, her interest in the topic clear.

"Yes, my gentleman caller was Patrick Godsend, Pastor Godsend's grandson. You spoke briefly with him, didn't you?"

With a long sigh and a gentle hum, Julia nodded. Her gaze was dreamy as she stared at the far corner of the room. "Mmm hmm…I sure did. Oh, what a fine speaker he is. Why, he never said one improper or impolite word! It was a true pleasure to have a word with him—even if the word was just a short one. My oh my, I wouldn't mind getting a chance to get to know that feller a little bit better—"

Julia's eyes widened, looking like half-dollar coins in her pretty face. Color rose in her cheeks as she whirled to face Kristen.

"I didn't mean—I, uh, I just meant—it ain't—no, it

isn't—oh! Why oh why don't I know enough to keep my big mouth shut when it shouldn't be open? My mama always said if anything got me in trouble it would be my mouth and by God she was right, wasn't she? Oh, Kristen, I didn't mean no disrespect or..." Julia's words trailed off helplessly in the face of the laughter that greeted them.

Kristen waved away the dancer's apology. "Stop it, you're fine. Just fine, really. Your mother would be wrong in this case, my friend. You're not in trouble, not by your mouth or anything else. Why, there's no need to apologize for saying what's on your mind. And what woman wouldn't want the chance to spend time conversing with a polite, intelligent man—especially one who's as handsome as Patrick?"

Julia's brow creased. "You mean you don't mind my being interested in the preacher's grandson? But I thought he was interested in you. I could see it plainly in his face, that he holds you...that he, uh, that he..."

There was no stopping the mirth that bubbled to the surface, so Kristen didn't try. Besides, it felt good to laugh.

Geraldine watched the exchange over her needlework with raised eyebrows and a big grin. She looked from one woman to the other, shaking her head so hard her thick, shiny curls bounced with each quick movement. The scent of the rosewater she used to rinse her hair filled the room. It made Kristen think, yet again, of her mother's rose garden.

But laughter forestalled any homesick feelings she might have had otherwise. The confusion on Julia's face made her laugh still harder, though she knew she shouldn't. Since she had no romantic leanings whatsoever for Patrick, it seemed wholly ridiculous that anyone would ever imagine she did.

Finally she caught control of her funny bone. Kristen sucked in a deep breath, and then exhaled slowly. "You think I have an interest in Patrick, don't you?"

Julia nodded.

"Well, put the notion right out of your head. I don't have any interest in the man—other than as a friend, of course. He's smart and kind, and good company, but we aren't romantically involved." There. That should put the other woman's mind to rest.

It should have done so, but apparently it didn't, because Julia asked, "But how could you not?"

"I just don't fancy him in that way." It seemed obvious, and logical, and the words slipped easily from her tongue.

"But he's sweet on you. It was real clear when he asked for you at the door that he holds you in high regard. *Very* high regard. "

Julia pulled her needle through fabric with less attention than she had earlier. It was almost a given that the stitch would need to be pulled out, but Kristen kept quiet.

So many aspects of life were different here in the west. The whole concept of courting and romance seemed miles apart from what she was used to. However could she hope to find a husband when she so patently didn't understand the rituals and rules associated with keeping company here?

She didn't want to insult the other woman. It was clear Julia was very interested in Patrick and saw him as relationship-worthy. Still, she had to make it equally clear that he held no romantic attraction for her.

"I know that Patrick thinks he's sweet on me, but that doesn't mean we're well suited for each other," she explained with as much diplomacy as she could conjure on such short notice. "Just because a man likes a woman, it doesn't mean she holds the same feelings for him, does it? I mean, you must have felt the admiring glances of many men, especially while you're dancing in the show. It doesn't mean you fancy every man who looks your way or smiles at you, does it?"

"It most certainly does not." Geraldine pulled a face, crossed her eyes and stuck out her tongue. "*Blech!* Half of the men who hoot and holler at me just give me a case of the heebie-jeebies, that's what they do. Julia knows as well as anyone that just because a feller ogles you, or even sees you as more than a gal on stage in a pretty costume, it doesn't mean he's your destiny. Right, Julia?"

"Right. But the men who pay to watch us dance...well, Patrick's not like any of them." Kristen heard the catch in her friend's voice when she said the man's name, and it pulled at her heartstrings. Somehow Julia had fallen hard, and fast, for the preacher's grandson.

"Patrick's just a man," Kristen said. She didn't want Julia to get hurt if Patrick didn't return her feelings, so she wasn't about to build him up any higher than Julia had already done. "He's the same as all men are, more or less. My Aunt Irene used to say that men are like gloves and every woman's hand is built for a certain glove. The hard part is finding a pair to fit every finger on your hand." She looked down at her own hands. "I know it's not romantic, and may even be a bit silly, but I loved my aunt and keep the image firmly in my mind. I believe my heart will know when I've located the gloves made for my hands... I promise you, Julia, that Patrick Godsend isn't my pair of gloves. He's certainly well-made and of superior quality, but he's not for me."

"You sure about that?" Julia asked breathlessly. "You're not just saying that to make me feel better?"

Kristen shook her head. "I wouldn't do that to you—or to Patrick. From the bottom of my heart, I'm sure that Patrick and I are not hand-and-glove suited for each other. So, he's a free man, open to any and all women interested in him."

"Thank goodness!" Julia swept a hand across her brow, wiping away the sheen of perspiration that had gathered on her smooth skin. She smiled so broadly every dazzling white tooth came into view. "I was afraid you took to him as much as he takes to you." Suddenly her expression turned sober. "Ohh..."

"What's wrong?" Geraldine was busy embellishing her flower but the sound of the woman's moan brought her gaze up. "Julia? Are you ill?"

"No, I ain't—ah, I am not ill. I'm just...well, I just remembered that even though Kristen doesn't favor Patrick in a romantic way, he still has it in his mind that he cottons to her. And what chance do I have against a mind that's already made up, especially when the lady in mind is so elegant and I'm so ordinary?" Her lower lip quivered.

Kristen rushed to think of something to soothe Julia's emotions but Geraldine spoke before anything came to mind.

Geraldine snorted, the. sound cutting the tension.

"Aw, honey, don't give one ounce of concern to a man who says he knows his mind. Take it from me, sister…men know their own minds only when we tell them what they know. Until then, it's all a muddle for them. Really, I've seen it before…a woman holds much more power over a man than even she knows." She dropped her embroidery onto her lap and wiggled her fingers to work out the stiffness. "And a smart, pretty, cheerful gal like you? Shucks, any man would be lucky to have you tell him his mind. Believe me, Julia—that Patrick will come around to seeing who you are as soon as the stars fall out of his eyes. Then, his eyes, his mind and his heart will belong to you."

"You really believe that?" Julia asked.

Geraldine nodded. "I do. That is, if the two of you are each other's destiny. Then, he's all yours—and, for better or worse, you're his. That's the way love works."

"Amen," Kristen whispered.

Chapter Fourteen

The sun hung low but Jack wasn't going to be deterred by the hour. He had a mind to see Kristen, and one way or another he was going to do so. There was still plenty of time for a short walk along the creek, at least an hour or two before dusk crept out of its hiding spot and covered the land.

He strode along the sidewalk. Morning shoppers had given way to early saloon-goers and tired miners, so he dodged dirty men dragging packs instead of young women with babies.

It weighed heavy on his mind that once his business with Brown was done, he would head back to Kansas and leave her here by herself. Oh, sure, she seemed to have made friends with some of the revue girls, the lady who ran the boardinghouse and, of course, the preacher's grandson but were they enough? A bunch of women and a Bible-carrying drifter—how could they possibly provide the type of protection a woman might need in such a rough environment?

Jack chuckled. He had forgotten that Kristen was no ordinary woman, and seemed perfectly capable of taking care of herself. Why, he had never met a woman with such an independent streak before. It was a quality he had never considered attractive in women but it suited Kristen well.

She hid something. He knew it as well as he knew

his own name. But what? What could she keep so close to her heart that she wouldn't confide in him?

A man. It had to be a man. What else would she try to hide?

The boardinghouse lay just on the other side of the road. He waited while a buckboard passed, then stepped out into the wide street. He had only gotten a foot from the walkway when he heard his name called from behind him.

Had he been a swearing man, he would have sworn. Twice he'd tried to take Kristen walking by the creek, and both times his plan was thwarted—by someone calling him. For a man who was new in town, and knew hardly anyone at all, he sure spent a whole pant load of time answering to folks.

Jack stopped and looked over his shoulder.

Great. Just the person I didn't want to see.

He stepped back onto the walk and nodded. "Godsend."

"Sterling." Patrick tipped his hat.

He shifted the bundle to his left hand and held out his right. Grudgingly Jack shook it, a tense up-and-down snap that lasted scant seconds but it seemed to satisfy Patrick.

"Just the man I hoped to see." Patrick's voice was friendly but there was an undercurrent to his words.

Jack couldn't believe his misfortune. He'd already dealt with Brown this morning. It seemed completely unfair to have to wrangle with Godsend in the same day.

Life isn't fair. Granddad had hammered the words into Jack's head from childhood, and he recalled them now.

He'd always realized that Granddad was right, but he had never liked unfairness in any situation. It seemed to him that if a man did the right thing—or tried his best to do what he knew was proper—then everything else connected with the issue should be fair and equitable. He spent his adult life trying to be just in his personal and business dealings but, as he was reminded yet again, doing the right thing didn't insure the fairness of a situation—or of life.

There was an expression in Patrick's eyes…something new that gave the man an exaggerated air of confidence. Jack couldn't put his finger on what, exactly, was different but, as he stared into Patrick's eyes, he was pretty sure he didn't care for it.

When he got right down to it, it wasn't Patrick Godsend, the man, who annoyed Jack. Rather, it was Patrick Godsend, Kristen's suitor, who rubbed him the wrong way. He had no claim on Kristen, but that didn't mean he wanted anyone else to claim her. And this preacher's grandson? Instinct told him he wasn't the right man for Kristen—not by any stretch of the imagination.

The surest way to get something out of the way was to tackle it head on, and the faster he and Patrick concluded their little sidewalk meeting the sooner Jack could see Kristen.

He plastered a smile on his face, and asked, "Oh, really? Why is that?"

"I thought we should have a…well, let's just say I think it's high time you and I have a little chat." Patrick motioned to a vacant spot beneath the sundry shop's awning. It provided just enough shade for the two of them to step into, so they did.

"I don't know what you and I have to discuss, and I'll be quite frank…I've got a pressing engagement so my time is limited." Jack forced himself to remain cordial, although the command performance discussion rankled him. Even a polite man has a breaking point, and Patrick was edging dangerously close to pushing Jack to his. "I'll give you a few minutes, but that's all I can spare. What's so all-fired important that you hijack me on a public street?"

A muscle worked in Patrick's jaw. Jack noticed the man was freshly shaved, and scented with aftershave lotion.

He swept a palm across his own cheek. It, too, had been shaved by the barber earlier in the day but all traces of the lotion the man had slapped onto his cheeks had dissipated hours earlier. The bathing facilities in the back of the stable, where he rented a cot, were rudimentary. Standing beside Patrick he realized just how far down his standards of hygiene had fallen since he'd been in town. He was bathed, and somewhat freshly shaven, but the fastidiousness about his person he took for granted back in Kansas had vanished in the rough-and-tumble reality of life in the western frontier.

It irked him that the other man looked better than he did, and was more presentable. It especially bothered him that Patrick smelled good.

When he didn't get an immediate response, Jack asked, "Well? You've got me here. What do you want to talk about? Make it quick, won't you? What is it, man?"

"Kristen."

The word silenced the bustling world around them. Miners' boot steps scuffling along the walk, donkeys and horses *clip-clopping* on the street and even the sound of raucous laughter coming from the saloon doorway dropped away.

Her name, spoken in the other man's voice, made Jack's world stand still.

Jack had no trouble finding his footing in business affairs. Never had, and hopefully never would. But the affairs of the heart were an entirely different matter. Not only did his feet feel like the world beneath them was as uncertain and slippery as a half-frozen stream, the legs attached to them felt nothing like the sturdy tree trunks he'd grown up on.

A good bluff worked well in certain situations. Jack decided to try one now.

"Kristen? I hardly think there's anything to discuss on that front."

Patrick eyed him suspiciously. "Are you saying you don't have any interest in Miss Marsh? Is that it?"

Jack shrugged. "I'm not saying anything one way or the other about her, my man. All I'm saying is that you and I don't have anything to discuss where she's concerned. Now, if you'll excuse me, I've got business to attend to."

The hand on his forearm surprised him. Not only had the other man reached for him with lightning-fast speed, his grip was tight and firm. Jack looked down at the hand, saw the way its veins stood out clearly and wondered where a preacher's kin could have learned to be this assertive—or move so quickly.

He looked up. Their gazes locked. They stayed that way for several heartbeats, neither one willing to blink or break contact.

"I suggest you remove your hand, Godsend. Now."

The hand fell away. "We need to talk, Sterling. Now."

The man's gutsiness impressed Jack, even though he didn't want anything about Godsend to make an impact on him. He would have greatly preferred to walk away, find Kristen and continue his day but that was, obviously, not going to happen until he put this small detour in its place.

Calling on his reserves of patience, Jack leaned against the wall behind him and crossed his arms over his chest. "Your granddaddy must have taught you about tolerance. A man only has so much tolerance for anything—or anyone. I'll be honest, you're pushing me to the limit, so you'd best say whatever it is you're all fired-up to say and have done with it."

Jack saw the man's Adam apple bob up and down. Then he noticed the lines radiating from the corners of Patrick's eyes, the straight line his lips formed while he contemplated his words and the serious, almost deadly, stare in his eyes.

It hit Jack all at once. Patrick Godsend wasn't merely infatuated with Kristen—he loved her.

He would have lost the contents of his stomach had he been another, less proud and self-controlled, man. He swallowed harder than Patrick had, and tasted the sting of bile on his tongue.

"My granddaddy taught me a lot of things. I've heard him preach from the time I was a baby, so I've had more than enough lessons about life drilled into my head. Endless lessons on tolerance...faith...the evils of sin and the rewards of righteous behavior..." He stared into Jack's eyes and finished, "...and love. Granddad taught me about love, and about how to treat a lady."

Jack hardly knew what to say. The man spoke with his mouth but the words came from his heart.

"It sounds like you've been taught all the important things, then."

"I think so." Patrick took a deep breath, and then asked, "Do you love her?"

The question was unexpected, but then everything about the meeting was unusual. Jack evaded giving an honest answer by stating the obvious.

"You do. That much is clear."

Without hesitation, Patrick acknowledged his feelings. "I do." Some of his vigor ebbed, and his chin dropped slightly. His deflation seemed to make his broad shoulders shrink. He pressed, "But do you? Love her, I mean."

Jack refused to be cornered, even by someone he was quickly learning to respect. How he did—or did not—feel for any female in town was no one's business save his own.

"My feelings belong to me until I decide to divulge them." He smiled, hoping to put an end to the conversation. "Now if you'll excuse me—"

Patrick's hand shot out again, but Jack was prepared this time. He sidestepped the grasp, shaking his head disbelievingly. "That worked once but I don't suggest you try it a second time. I might not be as amiable to being held up as I was a minute ago. It would be wise for you to remember that."

"Point taken. I apologize for my rude behavior. I don't know what I was thinking."

Patrick let his hand drop to his side. He clutched the small bundle he held so tightly the string holding it closed tore one edge of the brown wrapping paper. It was a small rip but it pulled the paper open wide enough to expose a flash of yellow.

Tearing his gaze from the rent in the bundle, and pulling his mind from thoughts about fripperies designed to woo females, Jack brushed aside the apology. He felt sorry for the other man, and suddenly he wasn't as anxious to be done with him as he had been only moments earlier.

"Don't apologize." Jack reached up, removed his hat and slapped it against one thigh. Dust flew into the air, so he waved his free hand to clear it. After he'd put his hat back in place, he smiled—one of those between-men smiles that women aren't ordinarily privy to. "Listen, we all know how a woman can tie a man up in knots. They're supposed to be the weaker sex but by God, the joke's on us, isn't it?"

Patrick released a shaky breath. He chuckled, and then said, "Amen to that. My grandfather, being a pastor and all, has seen a lot of life."

"I'll bet he has," Jack said. He could only imagine all the things—both good and bad—a man of the cloth might encounter.

"Well, he's always said that God made women stronger than any man living could ever dream of being."

"Smart man, your grandfather."

"He surely is." Patrick warmed to the subject, and managed a tight smile. "You know, I always figured it was the bit pertaining to childbirth that he alluded to, but now that I'm of an age where I'm courting, I'm beginning to see what he meant all these years. Just when I think I know my own mind, a woman, so slight I could pick her up and twirl her about, changes it for me with not much more than a turning of one slim shoulder. Can you believe that?"

Jack's own mind felt like it had been made and remade so many times his head ached.

"I surely do. And the funny thing is, any woman you might want to pick up and twirl can only be twirled if she allows it." Jack gave a conspiratorial wink. "I've had a mind to twirl a few ladies in my time but I've never been stupid enough to do so without first asking permission."

"I knew you and I would see eye to eye, Jack." Patrick pushed his hat back on his head. He ran a thoughtful finger along his temple.

Jack saw his hair had been greased and parted, and it, too, had been scented. Together with the package and aftershave, the only conclusion to be drawn was that Patrick was prepared to call on a woman. But if not Kristen…then who?

Chapter Fifteen

Relief coursed through Jack's veins when Kristen answered his knock on the boardinghouse's front door. Despite the late hour, she looked fresh. It took every ounce of self-restraint he had not to lean forward and bury his head in her golden hair, inhaling the sweetness of her the way he would a hothouse lily.

A smile spread slowly across Kristen's face. The way her bow-shaped lips pursed did wondrous things to his heart.

Take your eyes off her mouth, man! You're here to court her, not devour her!

"Jack. What a pleasant surprise." She did not invite him in, nor did she step out onto the porch.

"I hoped you might think so," he answered, praying his pounding heart was recognizable only to his own ears. It was strange, the way she kept her body in the doorway. Usually a caller received an invitation to enter, or at the very least a hostess might come outside to chat for a few minutes. But this...half in and half out...

Jack didn't have long to consider the meaning behind her behavior. Kristen wasted no words pretending she was something she wasn't.

"So, you've come to your senses, have you?"

Her words made him feel like an errant child. He'd forgotten his ridiculous behavior. So much had happened since they sat together in the makeshift park that he'd put her dashing away from him completely out of his mind.

Time to pay the piper.

"I did show my childish side in the park, didn't I?" He had removed his hat before knocking on the door. Now he held it earnestly over his heart.

"You did." Kristen's tone was teasing, her laughter barely concealed.

So he wasn't completely in the doghouse! Jack pressed his luck, and raised one eyebrow in question.

"Any chance you'll look kindly on this poor man's misdeed? Any hope you'll just think 'Poor Jack, he spoke without thinking'?"

"'Poor Jack'…if memory serves me right, the whole 'Poor' thing is what set you off."

Her lips twitched as she struggled to remain serious. Jack was mesmerized by the way they pulled together, so soft and tender looking, and oh-so pink. He longed to reach a finger out, and trace the outline of her smile.

He remembered himself, and cleared his throat, then shrugged. "You make me sound like a bundle of dynamite. I admit, I spoke out of turn but I don't think I blew my stack or acted too harshly."

Capitulation came easily. "You're right," Kristen answered with a grin.

She stepped out onto the porch and closed the door behind her. When she walked over to the porch railing, he followed. She perched on the rail, one delicate hand wrapped tightly around the top railing, and went on, "Your green-eyed behavior was actually pretty amusing. I didn't realize a man of your apparent good breeding could fly into such a jealous snit."

"*Snit?* I did no such thing." He sputtered over the words. No one had ever accused him of being jealous before, but he didn't want to dispute that point. In his heart, he recognized it as the truth. But the snit comment…that he took umbrage to. Rather than have her storm off again, he changed tactics. Thinking fast, he teased, "Besides, isn't a snit something a woman wears to the theatre? Or, let me see…I know! A snit is the place where birds find food for their young, isn't it? No, no…that's not right… Hmm, I seem to recall hearing somewhere that a snit is one of those European horse—"

"Stop! I give up!" Kristen clutched her middle, laughing so hard she teetered on the railing. He reached a steadying hand out, holding lightly onto her upper arm until she got herself under control and waved him away. "You're a funny man, Jack Sterling. I like that— a sense of humor—in a person, so I'm going to overlook your—"

He held his right hand up, palm facing her, and cut her off. "Don't say it! I don't want to hear the word again, if you don't mind." He dropped his hand, laughing, and sat on the railing beside her.

"Fine, I won't say it."

Her cheeks were rosier than usual, the laughter bringing a full bloom to her face. Jack could have sat and stared at her all day long but that wouldn't be wise. Sooner or later, he would want to kiss her.

Better stick to the plan.

He stood, brushing his palms down his thighs to wipe away the moisture. "I wondered if you would consider taking a walk with me. Not far," he rushed to add when she looked up at the sun. "Just down to the creek. It's cooler by the water, and much more pleasing than strolling along these dusty sidewalks."

Just then a horse *clip-clopped* by, the buggy it pulled clattering over the uneven lane as noisily a locomotive off its tracks. The contraption was so deafening, they had to refrain from speaking until it passed.

He smiled. "See? Too loud here for two people to have a civilized conversation. So, what do you say? Are you up to a stroll by the creek? I promise to have you back before Mrs. King puts dinner on the table."

Emotions flitted so quickly across her face that it seemed she considered, discarded, and reconsidered a multitude of options in mere seconds, much like a butterfly choosing which flower to light upon

Finally, she nodded. "Let me get my bonnet."

****

A gentle breeze blew off the water, fanning her cheeks and lifting the hair on the nape of her neck. Kristen untied her bonnet, and then pulled it off her head. She tied the ribbons, dangling the bonnet from her fingertips as they walked.

"Lovely, isn't it?" A cottonwood branch had fallen into the center of the creek, forming a natural diversion for the water to follow. Some of the current parted around the branch; a gentle spray flew up and over the highest part of it. A miniature rainbow shone in the mist.

"Yes, it certainly is." Jack's tone caught her attention, and she tore her gaze from the rainbow to look at his face. As she suspected, her companion wasn't gazing at the creek, the branch or the rainbow.

Instead, he stared down at her, a small smile playing at the edges of his lips.

Uh-oh.

"The rainbow, Jack." She pointed to the creek. "Do you see it?"

He smiled fully. "I see it. It's nice." Removing his hat from his head and slapping it against his thigh, a habit of his she had come to recognize, he gave her a thoughtful, almost appraising, glance. Then he looked over at the creek before he brought his gaze back to hers. "Yes, it's nice, but it's not, by any stretch of the imagination, the prettiest sight down here this afternoon."

The compliment was sweet, and since he didn't seem to expect any reply, she simply returned his smile. When Jack reached for her bonnet, she gave it to him. He laid the bonnet and his hat on the end of a fallen log beside them, and then held his arm out before them. Kristen took the silent invitation, and continued strolling along the creek bank.

"Much more pleasant to walk without having to tote our belongings, isn't it?" His conversation was so ordinary, so harmless and non-demanding, it put Kristen at ease.

When they first arrived at the creek, and she had glanced at the spot where she and Patrick had sat on the picnic blanket, a wave of apprehension hit her. It was fast-moving, though, and gone almost before she realized it had arrived. Jack and Patrick were different men, and even if the location was the same, her feelings and theirs as well would make this a very different outing. Wouldn't it?

"It is." Her hands swung at her sides, and she felt

lighter without having to drag her bonnet around with her. "And I don't believe there will be much other foot traffic here this late in the day, so I'm sure our things are perfectly safe back there on the log."

"I believe you're right. I haven't heard of any hat thieves or bonnet rustlers lurking about since I've been in town." Jack's smile made the sun seem dimmer by comparison. She loved it that he smiled so often, and joked so freely.

"Nor have I."

They strolled slowly, enjoying every minute of the quiet. Neither was in a hurry, their steps evenly matched. A lark sang out, and Kristen offered the information she learned from Patrick about the bird.

"Now that bird has some admirable traits," Jack said with a nod. "Leaving when it feels closed in, not wanting anyone else to encroach on what belongs to it and being more concerned for caring for its family than its own well-being—well, that's just the kind of bird I think I'd like having in my backyard. Sounds honest, and I like that in birds. People, too."

Kristen's spine stiffened. Under normal circumstances, honesty was a trait she held in high esteem, as well. But these weren't ordinary times, and while she hadn't out-and-out lied to Jack she had been evasive. Guilt pricked her—but not enough that she was willing to come clean with him and own up to her lies-by-omission.

Better to change the subject.

"I've been giving lessons to the revue dancers. They all live at Brown's Rest, so it's no trouble to schedule classes around their dance programs."

Jack looked momentarily annoyed that she had

broached a new topic, but he quickly recovered. He seemed interested when he asked, "What sort of lessons do you give? Bird identification lessons?"

She smiled, thankful he hadn't pressed the honesty point and even more grateful for his fast, witty repartee.

"No, I don't give birding lessons." She poked Jack in the upper arm. It was a quick gesture but she felt the muscle beneath his shirt, the hardness of his body, in that one small touch. Forcing her attention from Jack's muscles and onto the girls and their lessons, she said, "I teach them about speaking properly, coaching them on both delivery and sentence formation. Also, I instruct them on some of the, ah, finer points of keeping house. You know, dealing with servants and household accounting, that sort of thing."

"Do you think the dancing girls will have need of those talents? I have to be honest here," he glanced down at her but Kristen kept her gaze fixed on the uneven ground at her feet. The last thing she wanted to do was stumble and fall into the creek! Too, not looking at Jack when he talked about honesty didn't bring a blush to her cheeks. "I have yet to meet a revue dancer who has a houseful of servants under her care. And, one step further than that, I've never heard one of those revue dancers utter a single, solitary word from the stage. So, are you sure the lessons shouldn't be in something they can use, like the newest dance steps from...oh, I don't know...New York or Boston, maybe?"

"Excuse me?" Kristen's heart skipped a beat.

"Dance lessons. You know, the newest steps and all. I just figure they might be more useful than the servant angle. And since you're from back east, I just thought you might be the go-to gal on dancing, that's all."

She refused to rise to the bait. With as innocent a smile as she could muster, Kristen turned to Jack and said, "Oh, but you're mistaken. Most of these ladies aren't going to be dancers forever. They're going to move on and find new lives for themselves. I'm just helping them prepare for what lies ahead."

"So they can leave the past behind them?" The meaningful stare he gave her made Kristen uneasy but she held her ground.

"That's right. I'm going to help them do just that. And if they never choose to divulge their pasts, no one will suspect what they've done or where they've been because they will be ready and able to take on new challenges." She swallowed, her throat feeling much tighter than it should, before she lifted her chin. "A woman should have choices in this life. I'm just giving the revue dancers some choices. There's nothing wrong with that, is there?"

He shook his head. "No, there isn't."

Whew! Now to change the subject again…

"I'm glad we agree. Now, on a more pleasurable note, I've begun giving embroidery lessons in the afternoons, as well. There will be watercolor painting lessons in the future, if the stitching is ever successfully mastered. At this point, it's anyone's guess whether some of the ladies will sew without leaving blood spots on their work, but at least we're enjoying ourselves. That's important, I think. To enjoy what you do."

"Mmm hmm…"

Leave it to him to suddenly close up like a clam at low tide. Kristen wanted to keep the conversation going smoothly, to keep Jack's mind so well occupied he wouldn't be able to formulate any other probing questions.

"Do you enjoy your work? Do you like owning a sawmill?"

He stopped walking, so she had no choice but to do the same. They had reached a bend in the stream. A cluster of large cottonwoods hung low, providing dense shade and welcome coolness.

"Very much, although I don't wonder if I'm biased because I've never done anything else. I've nothing to compare what I do there against what I could do elsewhere." He pondered a moment more, and then added, "But since I'm content, I suppose it doesn't matter that I've only attempted one profession. The roundabout answer is yes, I do enjoy what I do. Sorry it took so long to get to the point." His quiet laughter blended flawlessly with the sound of the burbling creek water.

"You got to the point, and that's all that matters."

She fanned her face with one hand while she looked around for a place to rest. Another log, longer and wider than the one where they had left their hats, was just a few feet away. With a nod in its direction, Kristen asked, "Do you mind?"

"Not at all. I could use some time off my toes, too."

They sat on the log in companionable silence for a few minutes. It felt like they were the only two people in the universe and Kristen loved the thought. At that moment, she didn't need—or want—anything more than what she had beside her.

Just when she thought she might burst out in

unrestrained laughter from the sheer joy of the moment, Jack turned to face her. He stuck a hand in his jacket pocket and pulled out a small paper-wrapped bundle. He held it out to her.

"I saw these and thought you might like them."

Kristen hesitated. Back home, accepting a gift from a gentleman implied some social obligation. But here, where the world was wild and bundles were tied with butcher's string? Was it acceptable to take a gift from a man without having first agreed on their degree of entanglement?

She didn't care. Jack, and his gift, was the best parts of her life since she had left home. Whether or not being friendly with him, or taking his token, was socially acceptable or not wasn't worth the effort to consider.

Smiling her delight, Kristen took the package. It was light in her hand, so weightless it seemed impossible that anything could lay hidden beneath the paper.

"Open it," Jack prompted. Pleasure showed clearly in his eyes as he watched her undo the wrappings.

The earrings were simply made but elegant, with stones so vibrant they stole her breath. The turquoise seemed to glow as she ran a light fingertip across one earring. It warmed against her skin when she lifted them from the wrapping.

"Oh, Jack. They're beautiful."

"I hoped you might think so." Jack waited until she clipped them to her ear lobes before he went on. "My mother had a pair just like these. When I was a little boy and I'd try hard to remember my mother, I would picture her wearing the earrings and imagine her as a queen." He stopped, and then reached a fingertip to touch the left earring. His fingers brushed the side of Kristen's neck. His nearness raised gooseflesh on her arms but she hardly felt it.

"I'm touched beyond words." She stopped, wondering how to proceed. Never before had she received such a thoughtful gift, and she wanted Jack to know how much she appreciated the gesture. "I..." Kristen swallowed around the words caught in her throat, and then met his gaze. "I love them."

Jack's fingers spread along the back of her neck. He pulled her close as he leaned forward. Kristen's heart quickened when she realized what he meant to do but she made no attempt to avoid what seemed inevitable.

It was destiny, pure and simple. When Jack's tender kiss brushed across her waiting lips, she knew that every moment in her life had been leading up to this one, perfect kiss.

Chapter Sixteen

Julia held the length of yellow muslin up for inspection. Sunlight filtered through the parlor windows, making the fabric glow like gold.

"Isn't it the prettiest thing? Patrick is so sweet. Said it reminded him of me." Julia's voice held more than a hint of pride.

Since Patrick called upon her the previous afternoon, all anyone at Brown's Rest heard about was the visit, the man or what the man said, thought or did.

They all hoped the newness of the courtship would wear off in due time. Until then, Kristen did what everyone else had been doing; she smiled, listened patiently and nodded a great deal. She didn't mind, not really, half-listening to the chatter. It gave her plenty of time to reflect on her own adventure from the day before.

Jack had not tried to go further than the one perfect kiss, and for that Kristen was truly grateful. It was fine to be desired, but she had no interest in being pawed. Any man who wanted her body first had to claim her heart. Jack had done the first, but there seemed to be no way for their relationship to progress, and that stabbed like a knife to the quick of her. How could she give herself heart and soul to a man who intended to leave town at the conclusion of his business?

It seemed hopeless. But…the memory of their kiss

chased all other thoughts far from Kristen's mind. So far, in fact, she forgot to nod and murmur, something Julia quickly noticed.

"Kristen, are you all right? You seem awful quiet. Are you feeling poorly?"

"No need for concern. I feel fine, thank you. I just...oh, I guess I was just wool-gathering. Sorry."

"Aw, don't go apologizing to me." Julia carefully folded the yellow fabric into a small rectangle, and then hugged it against her chest. "I know I'm rattling on and on about Patrick. You must be getting tired of hearing me but you know I just can't help myself. That man...he makes my middle—oh I don't know how to explain it. He makes me feel all fuzzy inside, like I don't rightly know what I'm supposed to be doing. He makes me feel..."

"Fluttery," Kristen breathed.

"That's exactly right! I feel kind of fluttery inside, like I have a flock of sparrows locked up beneath my ribcage. Do you think that's normal, Kristen? I've never felt this way before, and I wonder if it ain't—oops! *if it isn't*—somehow strange. What do you think?"

With a small sigh, and a similar fluttery, caged-bird feeling, Kristen said, "I think it's absolutely the way you should feel when you've met someone special."

Julia's arms tightened, and she hugged the fabric closer. "Mmm...that's got to be it. That Patrick, he sure is something else..."

She squeezed Julia's shoulder as she brushed past her on the way to the front door. It was still early in the day, but Kristen planned to take a short stroll along the walkway. If she was lucky, she might run into her own someone special...

Just as Kristen placed her bonnet on her head and began to tie the ribbons, Julia started. Slapping herself on the forehead, Julia said, "I nearly forgot to tell you— a man came calling on you just before dinnertime yesterday. You were out, but he said he'd be back."

Slowly, Kristen turned to face the other woman. Feigning calmness, she asked, "A man? Did he give his name?"

"No name, but he did have an accent. Kind of eastern, the same as yours." Julia lowered her voice and grinned. "If it's any help, he was very good-looking. Tall, with a mustache, and dressed like a businessman. Suit, tie, polished shoes...looked out of place here in the land of the red dust, but he sure was a cool drink of water in the blazing sun. Land sakes, Kristen—you do know how to attract the handsome fellers, don't you?"

She smiled wanly. Yesterday's visitor could only mean one thing.

Suddenly the bright morning seemed dark and dismal. Wordlessly Kristen removed her bonnet. She turned and went up to her room, her mind working so fast negotiating the stairs was a challenge.

****

"Thank you for coming into my office, Jack. Please, be seated."

Randall Brown's message had come shortly after daybreak. Jack had taken his time shaving and dressing, not wanting to appear to be at the banker's beck and call. Too, he figured the land grabber might want to settle their differences in the fashion of the place, and if he was to take part in a gunfight before day's end he at least wanted to be groomed for the occasion.

But Brown didn't look like he wanted to fight. He

waited until Jack sat down before he sat heavily in the desk chair. For a long, tense minute neither man spoke.

Then, the banker plowed his fingers through his hair. It stood up at odd angles, and had his expression been less frustrated Jack might have grinned at the sight of him. But Brown's hangdog face, and the tense straight line he formed with his lips, discouraged glee.

"I don't know what to say." Brown spread his hands wide, palms up and fingers splayed. "This has never happened to me before, and I just don't know what to say about it. I'm shocked by what I've learned, what I've unwittingly been a party to. My father, and my grandfather, would be so disappointed if they knew…for once, I'm glad they're gone, not around to see my disgrace. I've brought shame upon my family, and upon myself. I am sorrier than I can say."

Jack recognized penitence when he saw it. He could also identify a man who wore the burden of mortification heavy on his shoulders. Randall Brown was a study in both.

"Why not start at the beginning? Tell me what happened. Maybe together we can figure out something to do about whatever it is."

Hope glimmered in the other man's eyes. Without a second's hesitation, he reached into the top desk drawer and pulled out a bundle of papers. A pulse hammered in Jack's temple. He recognized the parcel instantly.

"Before we talk, I think I should return what's rightfully yours."

****

Two hours later, Jack emerged from the bank with the deed in his breast pocket, just over his heart. He couldn't wait to place it in Granny's hands again.

A pang of guilt stuck him when he thought of his grandmother. How could he have doubted her grasp on reality? Granny was old, but she wasn't feebleminded. He would remember it in the future.

Perhaps a small gift, a token of the Wyoming Territory might please her. The Emporium had a nice selection of gee-gaws and frippery. It was still early. He had time to take a peek at the merchandise and choose something appropriate for Granny.

As he took a step off the walk and into the street, the bank's door opened again and the marshal stepped outside.

"That was quite a thing you did inside there, Mr. Sterling." Marshal Gifford looked carved from the same stone that made up the mesas surrounding Brown's Point. His skin was sun-toughened and his hair bleached. With the silver star pinned to his chest, Gifford looked every inch the western lawman.

"It was the right thing to do. I couldn't see pressing charges against a man who had been duped by one of his own employees. How could he know his assistant, the man he trusted implicitly to carry out his request to buy land at a fair and equitable price, was pocketing the cash and stealing deeds? Brown thought those deeds were bought on the up-and-up. If anyone's to blame, it's that snake he hired to buy property for him."

Marshal Gifford spat a long, brown stream of tobacco juice into the dirt. Then he wiped the back of one hand across his mouth, disgust on his grizzled face. "Mark my words, I'll blame that varmint all right—just as soon as I catch him. That snake can't get too far, not with the posse I intend to rustle up this very morning.

Yessir, that land robber will get what's coming to him."

"What more could I ask for?" Jack smiled, hoping to put an end to the conversation.

The lawman had more to say. "You could've asked for a whole lot more than you got, that's what. You could've made Brown pay damages, you know."

Jack shrugged. What good would that have done? Randall Brown had already had his dream of returning to the land where his family settled thwarted. Attempting to exact retribution seemed cruel, and unnecessary.

Jack had his deed. He didn't want anything else from Randall Brown.

"So, you planning on leaving town now? You don't have to, you know. We sure could use a feller like you around here." The marshal eyed Jack speculatively as he spoke.

Jack hurried to dismiss the offer. "That's kind of you to say, but I'll be heading back to Kansas. A few days, maybe…then I'll have to go home. My business is done here. I've no reason to stay."

"Shame. Well, good luck to you." Gifford spat again before he turned and headed toward the jail.

I don't have a reason to stay. Do I?

He turned, and squinted into the sun's glare. Brown's Rest was just at the end of the street. There were figures on the porch. Pulling his hat low and extending the brim with his open hand, Jack strained to see who stood there.

He recognized the first figure instantly. The sight of Kristen's slender waist, slight build and glowing hair brought an immediate smile to Jack's face.

Memories of yesterday, of feeling that girlish

143

figure pulled tightly against him, her arms locked around his shoulders and her heart beating next to his, made him want to rush across the street, onto the porch to lift her off her feet. Who was he fooling? All Jack really wanted to do was carry Kristen home to Kansas, introduce her to Granny and then, with the whole of Carroll's Junction looking on, marry her.

What's stopping me? I don't even care that she's keeping a secret. She can keep it, as long as she'll keep me, too.

His mind made up, Jack strode down the street toward the boardinghouse. There was no sense in putting off the inevitable. He had lost his heart to the woman, he might as well see if she felt the same way.

He had nearly reached the boardinghouse when what he witnessed stopped him dead in his tracks.

The man on the porch with Kristen swept her into his arms, leaned close and kissed her.

Jack watched the exchange for as long as he could tolerate it, his heart and head both ready to explode. Then, he turned on his heel and walked away.

He felt like he'd left his heart in the Wyoming dust. He was going back to Kansas, and he never planned on losing his heart again anyway so what did it matter if it stayed—crushed and broken—in the red soil?

Chapter Seventeen

Wade Gantry stood nearly a foot taller than Kristen, but even with his hat on his head he didn't look nearly as large in real life as he had appeared in her mind. When she had bolted, sure he and Father were insurmountable obstacles, Wade's presence in her life seemed stifling, overpowering and all-consuming.

Now, Wade looked perfectly ordinary. He wasn't a monster, wasn't someone to inspire fear or loathing, and he certainly wasn't larger than life. He was, quite simply, a man like any other.

When Julia announced a man was at the front door asking for her, Kristen knew in her heart it was Wade. There was no dodging his hold on her life any longer. No more running away. She must deal with him and be done with it. She hadn't wasted any time but had gone straight to the door—almost into Wade's waiting arms.

He removed his hat and held it loosely in one hand. Then, his gaze still fixed on hers, he placed the hat on the table beside the door. It seemed the logical place for hats, although Kristen thought it might be a more logical spot for a basket of flowers or something equally innocuous. Every time a man rested his hat on that table, trouble followed.

"Jane."

She hadn't heard her first name in so long it took her a moment to realize he addressed her. With a shrug, she supplied her middle name, "Kristen."

Understanding lit his eyes. "Ah, I see. Kristen, then."

Her night ruminations portrayed Wade as angry upon his arrival. Kristen released a pent-up breath, realizing for the first time she had been fearful of his wrath. She neither needed nor desired an ugly scene, so his amiable tone of voice was welcome.

"Wade."

A single footstep would have brought Wade close but he remained where he was. She was grateful for that, too.

"You look well." Wade acted as if they had seen each other at a party only days earlier, as if standing on the dusty boardinghouse porch in the middle of the western frontier was as acceptable as strolling across her father's lush lawn. "You don't seem any worse for the wear, my dear."

My dear. His term of endearment sent a shiver up her spine. Had he come to claim her after all?

Nonsense! I am not a piece of errant baggage, open to being carried off by just anyone. I will not be claimed—not now. Not anytime.

"Thank you." Letting the romantic name pass, she took a steadying breath and prepared to put an end to their involvement. "Obviously I didn't put enough miles between Boston and myself."

"Between me and you, don't you mean?"

The sky was a stunning shade of robin's-egg blue. Kristen took a moment to admire it, using the time to formulate an answer. Several retorts came to mind but instead of inciting an argument, she lifted her shoulders, and then let them slowly drop.

"I suppose I do mean just that." He seemed to take the comment well, so she pressed on. "How did you find me?"

A small grin, the kind they had been sharing for so many years, appeared on his handsome face. Kristen was reminded of Wade's kindness and intelligence, his fast wit and stellar business sense. He was a good man, and would make someone else a wonderful husband.

Honestly, she had been shocked to learn he was a willing participant in her father's scheme to form a business connection through their marriage. She would never have thought Wade would have agreed to it, but she had been dead wrong on the matter.

"It wasn't hard to find you. I doubt you could ever flee so far that I couldn't track you down." Had the words not been delivered with a smile she had seen so frequently in the past, and recognized as harmless, they might have been intimidating.

"Why, then?"

"Because I love you," he said softly. "It's that simple, my dear. I love you."

Now he took one step forward, closing the gap between them. Kristen stood her ground, and when Wade was nearly touching her she looked up into his eyes and saw the truth. He *did* love her. But how? And why?

As if he had heard the unspoken questions, he shrugged.

"But you and Father…it was a business arrangement, nothing more. Why, we both know it was, Wade! You and I, we've been friends—dance, croquet and pinochle partners—but we've never been romantically…uh, we've never been, well, you know…"

He grinned, wiggled his eyebrows, and then leaned down so his cheek was beside hers. "Close?"

The intimate expression brought instant heat to her face. Wade chuckled, running an idle fingertip across the apple of one cheek.

"You're blushing, my dear. Why, I haven't seen you blush this hard since the afternoon Fred Waterhouse fell into the Andersons' swimming pool wearing white linen trousers. Remember? When he emerged he looked nearly nude, didn't he?"

Kristen's face felt on fire at the memory. She wished she could control her embarrassment—or Wade's mouth. He teased her like a brother, something she had forgotten about. Normally she might have bantered back and forth with him, and had a few laughs. Now, she felt at his mercy.

"I'm sorry." Wade lifted her chin so their gazes locked, and she saw it was true. "I shouldn't tease you so. It's just that…well, you are particularly beautiful when you've got such high color in your cheeks. I am, frankly, taken by your beauty, dazzled by your brains and wholly impressed by your independence and determination."

"Wade…"

He shook his head, cutting her off. "No, please, don't stop me. Please, allow me the opportunity to speak my mind—and my heart. I've come a long way to see you, and I've got a strong feeling this is the only chance I'm going to get to say how I really feel about you."

"But…"

"Please. I need to do this. Please." He spoke

quietly, but his words carried weight. The time for teasing was past. Wade had something to say, and intended to say it, so she nodded. Best to let him get on with things, so they might settle their affairs once and for all.

"Thank you." He swallowed hard. "I admit that when your father first approached me about marrying you, it was with business in mind. He felt you would grow to love me and that you already had a soft spot in your heart for me so it shouldn't take long for that spot to grow."

"He was right. I do value our friendship."

Continuing as if he hadn't heard her, Wade said, "But I never viewed the arrangement purely as a business deal. You see, my dear, I have loved you for years. All the parties, the dancing and laughter, it all was real to me. I never would have agreed to marry a woman I didn't love, so saying yes to your father's plan didn't require any thought, not on my part, anyhow."

"I had no idea. Why, I thought—"

"You thought you were a business acquisition, not a life partner."

"Exactly."

Wade studied her face for a quiet moment, then asked, "And now that you know, does it change your feelings at all?"

She wanted to spare him, but she was done running from the truth.

"I'm sorry, Wade, but it doesn't. I am grateful for your friendship, but I don't love you. Not in…well, not in that way."

He considered the words. If there was any disappointment at the admission, he hid it well.

Finally he bent close, so close their noses touched, and said softly, "Indulge me…"

The kiss was brief, but tender.

When he pulled back, Wade kept his face near hers and stared hard into Kristen's eyes. She saw sorrow in his, and was sorry to be the cause of it.

"I will tell your father that we have, by mutual agreement, decided not to marry. I hope you don't mind if I tell him we will remain friends." He gave a hopeful smile.

Kristen nodded, feeling finally free for the first time in months.

"That's settled, then." Wade stepped away, put his hat on his head and walked to the steps leading down to the road. Halfway down, he paused and turned to face her. "Will you return to Boston? We all miss you there, and since we're not getting married there's no reason for you to continue running, is there? You don't have to decide now. Just think about coming back, won't you?"

While she wanted to throw her arms wide and proclaim her freedom to the blue sky above, it wouldn't be reasonable to make Wade feel bad about how things between them turned out. He was already being more than civil, and taking the unrequited love in stride, so she squelched her enthusiasm and just smiled.

"I'll think about it."

She watched Wade walk away without feeling regret over what she had turned away. He was a good man, but he wasn't the man for her. She knew it in her heart, and now that she and Wade had settled their affairs Kristen felt free to follow that stubborn heart of hers.

She stared thoughtfully into the distance as her

pulse slowed to a normal rate.

Patrick, astride a pretty Appaloosa, interrupted her thoughts. He dismounted, secured the reins to the hitching post, and then took the front steps two at a time.

He tipped his hat. "Good morning, Kristen. Nice day we're having, isn't it?"

"Just gorgeous. Julia's in the front parlor waiting for you. Just go on in."

Patrick opened the front door, holding it wide so she could enter before him. When she didn't move, he asked, "Coming inside? Or do you plan to go somewhere?"

An idea had been taking root in her mind since Wade's departure.

Why not?

"I believe I'm going to take a stroll. By the way, did you by any chance see Jack Sterling on your way down Main Street? Do you have any idea where he might be?"

Patrick grimaced, then stared sympathetically into her eyes. "I did. And I do." He paused, and then said, "I spoke with him, even. He, ah, he said good-bye, Kristen."

"Good-bye?"

"That's right. He's headed back to Kansas. I just saw him ride that big black horse of his out on the road at the far end of town."

Panic tore through her. Wasn't it just her luck that when she was finally able to love fully, the man she desired most would hightail it out of town?

"Your horse—Patrick, may I borrow your horse?"

Kristen hurried down the steps, grabbed the horse's

reins and leapt onto its back. Riding had been one of her favorite lessons at school, and she had several blue ribbons back in Boston to prove her skill as a horsewoman. While she preferred to ride side saddle, she was no stranger to sitting astride a horse. One summer of training—much to her mother's dismay—for an equestrian jumping competition had given her enough skill to sit almost any horse, in any manner.

She didn't wait for Patrick's reply. Instead, she turned the animal in a tight circle, pointed her in the right direction and dug her heels into the horse's flanks. They took off down Main Street in a cloud of dust.

The irony of her situation wasn't lost as she rode flat out down the road into the wilderness. Not so long ago she had ridden this same road, a runaway bride-to-be determined to find a new life for herself. Now she rode in the opposite direction, a woman with a life to call her own but no one to share it with.

If I didn't have bad luck with men, I'd have no luck at all. Oh, Aunt Irene, why didn't I see this coming? You always said I could "see" things, but this mess has certainly taken me by surprise!

The horse wasn't bred for running but it had heart. They were only about a mile or so out of town, but already the animal's breathing was labored. As much as she wanted to catch up to Jack , she couldn't do so at the horse's expense. She pulled back on the reins, slowing the horse to a gentle canter.

Disappointment combined with irritation tore a wail from her throat. Tears welled in her eyes but she was far too wound up to let them fall. There would be time to cry later on, time to catalogue her regrets and chastise herself for being too stubborn to see the truth.

She loved him. Pure, simple and as plain as the nose on her face.

As if sensing her frustration, the Appaloosa sped up slightly. Kristen realized the futility of her search. Jack could be anywhere by now. Trailing after him on a plow horse, without any supplies or a weapon to protect herself, was downright stupid. Every step further from town took her closer to losing her life to a band of Indians or any of the gangs of unscrupulous outlaws roaming the territory.

The spot where the stagecoach had been held up lay just beyond a bend in the track ahead. She would ride that far, and then turn the horse around.

I won't give up. I'll just go back and equip myself properly for the journey to Kansas.

It made sense, even though the thought of letting Jack put another mile between them tore a hole in her aching heart.

She pulled the reins tight and slowed the horse to a walk. It resisted at first, trying to keep the pace, but Kristen held firm.

Her mind raced as she considered, then discarded, plans. Perhaps journeying by stagecoach would be the safest and most economical way to go, but it would also take the longest and Kristen didn't want to waste a minute. She could either ride or go by coach to a railway station. It would be a faster trip but there was no guarantee that a train might go anywhere near Carroll's Junction, Kansas. What to do?

They rounded the bend in the trail, the horse finally having settled into its slower pace and Kristen's mind fully engaged on what lay ahead—figuratively. Had she been looking at what literally lay before her, she would have seen him before he spotted her.

The nickering sound of another horse caught her attention.

Kristen raised her head. She pulled so hard on the reins that the horse reared up onto its hind hooves before it came to a standstill.

Jack?

Or a mirage?

She stared hard, wondering if she might have lost her mind as well as her heart.

Then, she jumped down from the saddle and ran across the uneven ground toward him. She tripped over her skirt, and the rocks bit into the soft leather soles of her boots but she didn't care. It was Jack—and he was within touching distance!

Jack swung a leg over the pommel, and then dropped to the ground in one smooth, graceful movement. He moved so quickly he beat her to the center of the clearing.

With a low growl, he scooped her off her feet and hugged her tight against his chest. Kristen felt the warmth of his body. She inhaled the wonderfully masculine scent of him. Her fingers found their way into the silky curls at the nape of his neck.

She could have spent forever in his arms, but Jack abruptly put her down and held her at arm's length. Then, he dropped his arms to his sides and glared at her.

Startled by his reaction, Kristen stood and stared into his eyes. So many emotions danced behind the deep brown orbs she couldn't begin to identify them individually. For the first time since she had hopped onto Patrick's horse, she wondered whether she and

Jack could straighten their mess out.

"Jack?" His name became a question as it fell from her tongue.

Jack smirked, something she hadn't seen him do before now. The expression made him sinfully handsome but it was, nonetheless, unsettling.

"Kristen?"

His intentional mimic unhinged her further. She realized he was more upset than she imagined...

She didn't have to wait long to find out why Jack stared at her with such conflicted emotions etched into his face.

"Don't you have somewhere else you should be right about now? Isn't there some poor fool just waiting for you to kiss him?"

So that was it. He had seen Wade, and witnessed their kiss.

Kristen rushed to explain. There had been too many secrets between them in the past. Now it was time to clear the air for the last time.

"No, as a matter of fact, there isn't." She lifted her chin, ready to prove herself worthy of his trust. "You saw me on Mrs. King's porch a little while ago?"

Jack grit his teeth so tightly she feared he might crack them. He gave a sharp nod in response.

"I thought that might be it." Kristen reached out to touch his arm, but Jack sidestepped her. The movement hurt, but she refused to be deterred. "I can explain. I know how it looks, but—"

He gave a small snort of disgust. "You can't imagine how it looks. First you lure Patrick into thinking he's in love with you before you drop him like a hot potato. Then you keep company with me—did you forget you kissed me only yesterday evening? Good God, woman, it was only a few hours ago that you were in my arms! Then this morning I see you, out in plain sight, no less, on the boardinghouse porch kissing some stranger. They defy explanation, these escapades of yours!"

"That's where you're wrong," she insisted.

His face had gone hard at the telling of her "escapades".

"There *is* an explanation, for all of it. If you'll only listen to me, Jack, I can tell you the truth about everything."

He gave her a cold stare. "Well, wouldn't that be a novel idea? I tried more than once to get the truth from you, yet you kept avoiding it. I'd just about decided I didn't care what you were hiding when I caught you kissing that eastern dandy. Just tell me one thing… Is that man your husband? Are you married to him?"

"No!" Her hand flew to her chest, covered her galloping heart. "Wade's not my husband—and I'm not married to anyone, Jack. I've never been married, believe me."

"Who is he, then?"

She swallowed around the lump in her throat. Time to tell the truth—and pray the truth would set her free.

"He is—*he was*—my fiancé."

Jack considered her words. His features softened slightly, and her hopes lifted. She had never imagined one small, insignificant kiss could make him so jealous. If he only knew how little she felt when Wade held her.

If Jack only knew how her heart overflowed when she was in his arms…

"'Was'? I take it you two are no longer engaged?"

156

"That's right. We've broken off our engagement. That's what you witnessed on the porch."

Jack smirked again, but this time he looked almost amused. *Almost.*

They could have no future unless Kristen cleared the slate, and she knew it.

She didn't stop to think. She just plunged into her story.

"You keep asking where I'm from, Jack, and I just evade the issue. Well, I'm from Boston, and I escaped my situation the only way I could. I ran away from Wade, and my family, and the ridiculous marriage my father tried to force me into entering. I thought...oh, it doesn't matter what I thought, not now. What matters is the 'why' of things, you know?"

She looked to him for confirmation. When he nodded, she went on.

Ticking items off with her fingers, she said, "Why did my father encourage me to marry Wade? Because he knows Wade Gantry is a good, kind man. He believed I would eventually grow to love him. He meant well, but I couldn't abide his decision to decide my future."

She raised a second finger. "Why did Wade agree to marry me? That sweet man, he says he loves me. I believe he does, on some level at least, but one-sided love isn't foundation enough to build a marriage. Truthfully, I think Wade loves me more as a friend and dance partner than anything else. Once he's free of the engagement, he'll find someone who deserves his heart."

Kristen took a steadying breath before she raised another finger.

"Why did I become a runaway bride? Because I don't love Wade Gantry. Never have. Never will. And I believe marriage should be entered into with open, loving hearts—two of them. Mine? Wade didn't claim it."

She stopped speaking, suddenly out of words. They stood in the clearing for a silent moment as the reality of her confession sank in.

Then, it struck her that they stood on almost the precise spot where they had met. She flashed a small smile, feeling exposed and vulnerable but still hoping to smooth things over with Jack.

"Do you realize we met on this very same spot? It was right here that the stage was held up, remember?"

Jack removed his hat and plowed his fingers through his thick, dark curls. A lock fell over his forehead. Her fingers itched to push it back in place but she resisted the impulse.

True to character, he slapped the dusty Stetson against his muscular thigh before he positioned it back on his head.

"I remember," he said quietly.

"Pretty amazing that you just happened along at the exact moment we needed help, wasn't it?"

Jack didn't look pleased by the turn in the conversation. She had meant to find common ground, share a pleasant memory, but his grimace of displeasure returned. Kristen couldn't figure out why he looked like a storm cloud ready to burst.

"Listen, you're not the only one who's got some confessions to make." He swallowed hard, raked a palm over his cheek and adjusted his hat brim. She waited for him to go on. "I didn't 'just happen along' the day the stage was held up."

"No?"

"No. I planned to rob the coach that day, that's why I 'happened' along. My scheme was to stop it here, take what I was after, then leave. Of course, I hadn't planned on hurting anyone…merely stealing something. But then I found the coach was already being robbed, and you and the preacher were holed up in the middle of the shootout. What could I do?" He shrugged helplessly, as if the episode required no further explanation.

If the world had tipped sideways, Kristen wouldn't have felt more discombobulated than she did by Jack's admission. She shook her head in disbelief, wondering how she could have been so wrong about him. Was it possible she had no sense at all when it came to matters of the heart?

Her voice came out as a strangled whisper. "You…you're a stagecoach thief?"

She took a step back, putting distance between them. Still, she felt the weight of his confession pinning her heart down. The sensation was stifling, and she gasped for air.

"*No*. Of course not." Jack took a step closer, holding his hand out to her. This time, however, she avoided his touch. "How could you think that of me? Brown—Randall Brown—his assistant stole the deed to my grandmother's property. It was on the coach, in the strongbox. I only meant to swipe what was rightfully mine. It was stupid, I know, but I was angry. When I left Kansas, it was because Granny was heartbroken over the theft. I had to do whatever it took to make her happy again. Don't you understand?"

His eyes confirmed his words. They were clear and honest, and she believed him. When it came right down to it, Kristen was impressed that he'd taken such drastic measures to please an elderly woman. The world righted itself again. She breathed a sigh of relief.

Jack isn't a thief!

"I do." Then, she giggled. "So you're telling me you're a robber-turned-rescuer? Is that it?"

"I guess it is." He smiled, lightening the mood considerably.

Time for the plunge.

"Now what, Jack? Where do we go from here?"

He shook his head. "I thought I knew…"

Kristen's heart fell to her toes. She hadn't expected this, hadn't planned on what to do or say if he rebuffed her.

Jack gazed into her eyes for so long and so hard she thought he might never break the connection. When he spoke, his voice was filled with acceptance, and her heart lifted a little at the sound.

"When we met, I thought I couldn't afford to lose my heart to you. I figured since you're here and I'm going back to Kansas, ours had to be a platonic relationship."

She opened her mouth to interrupt, but he stilled her with a hand on her shoulder. He gave a gentle squeeze, so she let him continue.

"Then when I began to have feelings for you, I thought you were involved with Patrick. It ruffled my feathers, I'll admit, but I had to respect his claim on your affections so I stood back and watched your involvement. Remember, I knew I'd be heading back to Kansas before long."

Her mouth opened again, but Jack rubbed his palm along the top of her right shoulder so she stilled and enjoyed the sensation his touch brought.

"Then, when you and Patrick parted ways, I thought I might have a chance with you. I knew I shouldn't court you because of the Kansas thing, but by God you are irresistible. You drove me to distraction, and I couldn't help but want to be near you. Yesterday, by the creek…"

Jack hitched a deep breath, and then shook his head, a look of wonder on his handsome face. "I never felt that way about anyone before. Never."

"Me, either," she breathed.

Jack absorbed her words before he went on. "I thought I knew everything this morning—everything I had to know about Brown and the deed…Granny and the sawmill… Most importantly, I thought I knew what to do about you, and about me. About us. Then, I saw you with that stranger." He looked down at the ground for a moment, then raised his head and met her gaze. A small smile crossed his lips. "I got angry. I suppose you can see that when I get angry, I get on my horse and ride hard. Does that bother you?"

Surprisingly, it didn't.

"Not one bit."

"Good. There are a lot of things I can change about myself, but that's not one of them, I don't think. Still, if it bothers you, I could try to mend my ways."

"It doesn't. Don't change anything."

His hand had reached her exposed skin. While they spoke, he traced a slow fingertip along the nape of her neck. Gooseflesh rose on Kristen's arms. Every nerve ending was at attention, courtesy of his tender touch.

"I love you," he said softly. "I've loved you almost from the first minute we met, right here in that coach. But, there still remains one very large problem. I have to go back to Kansas."

He loved her! What else could possibly matter?

A wicked grin stole onto her face. "Are you afraid I'll cause a ruckus in Kansas? Embarrass Granny?"

Understanding made Jack handsomer than ever. "You mean you'll go back to Kansas with me?"

A nod was all she could manage. Tears of happiness pooled in her eyes.

Jack pulled her against his chest, holding her so tightly Kristen felt the air fly from her lungs. Finally, she was in the right set of arms, with the perfect heart beating against her cheek.

Jack held her away from him and stared intently into her eyes. He seemed to be considering something important, so she didn't tease or interrupt.

"I know this isn't the best place to ask, but Kristen, my love, will you marry me?"

She was glad she'd been wise enough to hold her tongue.

A single joyful tear dripped down her cheek when she nodded. "I will, Jack. And this place is just perfect—after all, it's where our love began."

A word about the author...

Sarita Leone loves walking on the beach, dancing beneath the stars, and writing romance.

She also loves hearing from readers, so contact her via her website:

www.saritaleone.com

her blog:

From the Heart, www.saritaleone.blogspot.com

or her Facebook page.

Thank you for purchasing
this publication of The Wild Rose Press, Inc.
For other wonderful stories of romance,
please visit our on-line bookstore at
www.thewildrosepress.com.

For questions or more information
contact us at
info@thewildrosepress.com.

The Wild Rose Press, Inc.
www.thewildrosepress.com

To visit with authors of
The Wild Rose Press, Inc.
join our yahoo loop at
http://groups.yahoo.com/group/thewildrosepress/